WHAT'S FOREVER GOT TO DO WITH IT

Sun Over Star Gazer Island, Book Three

DEBRA CLOPTON

What's Forever Got to Do With It

Copyright © 2025 Debra Clopton Parks

What's Forever Got To Do With It

Kat McConnell is tough, strong through and through—from the outside view... She owns restaurants from Corpus Christi Bay to Hawai'i, and yet she hurts inside, but no one sees it.

She lost the best friend and sister-in-law Olivia who was deeply loved by the entire family who've all suffered profound heartache from losing her. Kat's focus has been to be strong and encouraging for them while she throws`herself into her business.

Olivia wanted all of them to feel the love she felt in her short life with their brother, who has miraculously found love again like she wished for him. Now both of her sweet sisters have also. But not Kat, who is living more and more fully on the shores of Kona, Hawai'i, focusing on her restaurants and deep-sea fishing—which she loves as it helps relieve the stress and hurting heart she's hiding.

She's not expecting that when her dad, who owns one of the largest ranches in the state of Texas and also in Kona, which she never visits, hires a new manager, that the man will come to her restaurant to meet her. It is a moment Kat will never forget. Her heart instantly reacts to the tall cowboy with the look of determination in his green eyes—eyes that dig deep and yank her heart awake like she never expected.

What's forever got to do with it? Everything. Could she step out from behind her hidden heart and actually test love? Olivia is rooting her on from heaven above, but can Kat step out and trust, or will she push the want away and live life alone?

Once again, come to the shores of Corpus Christi Bay and take a side trip to the shores of Kona, Hawai'i, to find the healing heart of a cowboy waiting to find a new life—with Kat, if she opens her heart.

CHAPTER ONE

Rancher Clay Samson paused at the huge wooden arched entrance, unwanted unease slid through him—it had been a long time since he'd actually gone to a restaurant, especially one engulfed in the visibly romantic atmosphere of this place. Soft Hawaiian music drifted on the ocean breeze as he'd strode down the rough pavement toward the entrance of the Café by the Seaside. The obviously extremely popular restaurant sat on the edge of Kailua-Kona, and it radiated with the lively nightlife of the Hawaiian town on the bay.

His boss and friend, Mitch McConnell, had asked him if he would have dinner at his daughter's restaurant in town, introduce himself, and let her know she was welcome at the ranch, their family ranch. It had been a long time since she'd visited, her father explained. And he was right, Clay had been here for almost six months and had yet to meet Kat McConnell.

Mitch had told him she stayed very busy making trips to her restaurants on the islands and the Texas coast and hadn't visited their Hawaiian ranch in years. That was why he'd asked Clay to make a trip to town to introduce himself.

So, here Clay was, feeling uneasy but doing what had been asked of him.

As a man who loved ranching, Clay couldn't help but wonder why Kat would pick living in town instead of the hillside of the ranchland her family owned. There she'd get the best of both worlds, the view of the ocean and the calm of the land. The McConnell ranch in Texas was one of the largest ranches in the United States, and this one on the island was one of the largest on the islands. Not the biggest, but still amazing and with some of the best views available of the blue waters surrounding the island and views of volcanoes in the distance.

Cattle raised specifically on the island were to feed these people who filled this restaurant and others on the island. So her not visiting the ranch seemed odd. Especially now as he stood here at the Café by the Seaside, while the sun was setting on the edge of the ocean. Even from the entrance it was amazing.

Standing there feeling tense, and not because he was about to meet Kat, he just hadn't ventured out to dinner in a long time. Trying to relax, he focused on enjoying himself as if he were simply here among tourists. He already knew the food was great, since he'd looked up the reviews online and found Kat McConnell was obviously an outstanding chef.

There was inside dining and an outstanding dining area—outside drew him, so he'd made a late reservation. He'd also requested a table near the water's edge.

The host smiled as she came back to the desk. "Hello, cowboy, welcome."

He tipped his hat and returned the smile. "I guess if I'm coming to the coast, I should take my cowboy hat off and my boots too."

"*Oh no* you shouldn't. We love cowboys. You must be Clay."

"Yes. That's me. How did you know?"

"I took the reservation and remember that Texas drawl." Her smile widened.

"It gives me away all the time."

"In a very good way," she said. "Now, please follow me. I'm Lettie, and if you have any problems please let me know. I've got you a table at the front by the water next to the rocks where the gentle waves wash in. You'll love it. Do you have someone meeting you that I need to watch for?" She hitched a brow and added, "It's a very romantic spot."

"No," he said, startled by her question. "It's just me, but I hear the food is as amazing as the view."

"Absolutely," she said, smiling wider. "Especially now that the torches are lit up. You have one right next to your table with its flame sparkling in the evening view." She spun then and led the way through the smiling people sitting at the tables, enjoying themselves.

The sand was the floor and shifted under his boots as he followed the hostess to a small round table sitting at the end and edge of the deck. Waves washed in over the rocks below. A great spot that gave him a view of the entire place.

"How's this?"

"Perfect. Thanks." He sat down and took it all in.

"Enjoy, your waiter will be here soon." Then she walked away, but turned back. "I love seeing cowboys come down the hill for dinner. I used to work up there in Kona cowboy country then got this job with Kat McConnell. You're going to be glad you came down the mountain, the food is fantastic."

"I love it up there. Why did you come here?"

"Because of Kat and her amazing restaurants. You'll know once you've had her food. My plan is to move to Texas and work at one of her other restaurants, and that Texas slang of yours reminds me of the cowboys that will be there." She gave a wink, then went back to work.

He chuckled. The woman had a way and obviously Kat knew a great hostess when she saw one. He relaxed and looked around. There was an outside bar full of people sitting around it, eating and enjoying themselves.

All the tables along the deck, and the ones further back were all full. He took it all in and his gaze stopped at the view of the wooden swinging door right past the bar. It was in perfect line of view with his table. It opened as he studied it and a waitress came out, giving him a clear view into the busy kitchen before the door swung shut again.

He removed his cowboy hat, placing it in the empty seat beside him, the always-empty seat. Then he lightly tapped his fingers on the table to the beat of the song that the Hawaiian singer was performing beautifully. It had been a long time since he'd come to a restaurant to eat at night. Coming alone just wasn't the same...

His attention was drawn to the door of the kitchen when it opened again and he was startled to see the wavy red-haired lady walk out to stand in the space between the door and the bar. He recognized Kat McConnell instantly from photos at the main ranch house.

She now stood there surveying the restaurant. Her wild curling hair was pulled back in a low to the neck ponytail that moved as she placed her hands on her slim hips and scanned the area away from him. From the side he saw her smile as she turned slightly taking in all areas of the restaurant.

Clay couldn't look away. He had seen many pictures of his boss's daughters, all three of them were beautiful in their own way, but Kat had stood out with her wild red hair and wide smile. Her pictures as a young woman on the walls of the ranch were pretty, but now grown up and in person, she was stunning.

He mentally slapped himself on the side of the head, he wasn't here to look at or be impressed by the woman. He had *no* interest in any woman, especially his boss's daughter.

In that moment she slightly turned to take in his area of the restaurant and her gaze locked with his—instantly he felt like a cowboy getting bucked off a wild bull. Mentally he fought to hang on, but instead he hit the dirt in his mind, stunned by his insane reaction.

She blinked, looking startled too as if she saw him hit the dirt. Then her eyes flashed, her hand went to her neck as if to ease a knot in it.

A knot he felt in his own neck.

As if watching a movie he saw in her beautiful

expression the moment she kicked herself. Her expression grew firm, her eyes dimmed, she yanked her gaze off him, spun in the white sand and stormed back into the kitchen. The door swung closed behind her.

Completely floored by his reaction and hers, he yanked his gaze from the empty spot where she'd been and he focused on the water.

What had just happened?

"Would you like something to drink?"

The question pulled Clay's thoughts back, and drew his gaze to the Hawaiian shirt-wearing waiter with the name tag that said Sean. "I'll have a water, please."

"Would you want a drink from the bar also?"

"No, thanks." That was certainly something he didn't need, he needed his brain fully on track—not that it was, first he needed it to just come back on track.

After Sean went to get his water, Clay's gaze went back to the door of the kitchen. He'd come here to meet her—he had not expected his off-the-wall reaction.

Had his boss known this would happen? Surely not...

The odd thought rolled through his spinning brain

and he realized the last time he and Mitch met here to sign papers, and he was hired on, that Mitch had told him Kat was, as she often was, visiting one of her other restaurants. They'd viewed the ranch then eaten at one of the restaurants in Waimea near the ranch, and he'd talked a little about his family, the history of the ranch and children, their loss of their dear friend, who'd been his son's first wife, and how it had affected all of them.

Clay had shifted the conversation away from his own loss when Mitch tried to go there, and the understanding man hadn't pushed him forward. Though he had made it clear when he first offered Clay the job that he thought getting away would be good for him.

Now, Clay wondered if there was more to the offer? What?

Mitch had told him during their first talk that Matt, his son who'd lost his wife, had married her knowing he was going to lose her. But still, knowing he wanted her as his wife for a short time rather than never, he'd talked her into marrying him. Now, the thought struck Clay hard.

If he'd known he was going to lose Natalie, would

he have gone through the sorrow that still held him captive?

Yes. Absolutely.

The answer was quick. He'd have rather held her and loved her for a short while rather than never knowing the deep love that still held him in its wonderful, sometimes hard grasp. Time though had eased the pain to an internal loss that enabled him to have a life in other ways.

The difference was that Matt was now happily married again, and Mitch was happy about that and that his youngest daughters had found love also. It had hurt Mitch and his wife to lose their daughter-in-law and watching how hard her loss had been on all their adult children.

Mitch, who was his friend, now had a caring heart so here Clay sat, on the beautiful night with the moon shining bright as he tried to figure out if he should stay and eat or walk away.

He shook off the thought. He never walked away from anything and he wasn't doing it now.

He was one of the best cattlemen there was, and he

worked for the best one out there as far as he was concerned. They both respected each other even though there was a twenty-five-year difference in their ages. His boss knew his history. It was well known by all in the cattle industry, so when he'd declined the invitation to come to the wedding, Mr. McConnell had understood.

So, here he was, on the Island of Hawai'i, where the place gave him peace just like Mitch had thought it would. He'd told him on that visit that out of all of his family, Kat was the tough one. That she had no fear— or she *showed* no fear, he'd added at the end. That Kona and her restaurants were her escape and her peace places. But he'd added that he hoped, like Kat, Clay found Kona a place of peace.

Clay understood it now. And maybe that was why he'd thought it would be a good thing for him and Kat to meet, so here he was going to do as he'd been asked.

Sean came back with his water and asked if he was ready to order.

"What do you suggest?" Clay asked.

The young man grinned. "Kat McConnell is an

amazing chef. Her food is the best I've ever tasted. She's constantly trying new recipes, she comes up with at her apartment in town overlooking the ocean, where she starts creating them, and this restaurant is the one that gets to test them first."

"Sounds like a good plan." Either the young man had a crush on his boss or truly loved her cooking. Or both.

"So, here's the deal, we have our main menu, but we also offer things she's testing, and right now it's this *totally* amazing meal a cowboy would love. By your hat and jeans, I'm figuring you're a real cowboy from cattle country, either traveling or coming down the mountain and not someone just trying to look like a cowboy."

Clay laughed. "You've read me right, I'm a born and bred cowboy all the way."

"So's my boss and we get them as tourists but also from the ranches around here. The deal tonight is a steak and seafood dish that's got a tasteful Hawaiian twist to it. You might not know it but she's from Texas, so it has a Texas taste and a Hawaiian taste all together. It's an incredible blend. The steak is sliced before I bring it and layered with the seafood surrounding it, topped with a special sauce".

"I'll take it." It sounded too great so he didn't hesitate.

Sean nodded. "You're going to be glad you ordered it."

Clay was looking forward to trying a new creation by the woman he was here to meet. She actually needed to know he was the new manager at her family ranch, despite the tension he felt, he looked forward to tasting her new dish... He'd focus on that and not his reaction when their gazes locked across the deck.

CHAPTER TWO

Standing in her kitchen, Kat was still stunned by her reaction to the cowboy sitting at the far corner table. She'd been unable to look away from him and he'd looked shocked too.

Still shocked by the serious eyes locked with hers and the way her heart seemed to blow up inside her chest, she now stood motionless in the sanctuary of her kitchen.

It was the craziest, mind-blowing feeling she'd ever experienced and she'd been unable for a moment to look away from his beautiful emerald eyes. Eyes that clearly were as disturbed as she felt hers must seem looking at him.

Most might think feeling electric shock by a look was a romantic thing, *Crazy* was what it was to her, she *didn't* like the feeling.

Didn't like it at all.

She'd heard a lot of people talk about the first mind-blowing attraction they'd felt at some point—but she'd never felt it, never felt lightning bolt attraction. Until now.

Now in her safe place, her kitchen, she forced herself to concentrate on getting the dish she was creating right, perfect.

Sean, one of her waiters, walked in grinning. "You have a request for that amazing new steak and shrimp dish. The cowboy asked what I suggested and you know I loved that new meal. Plus, he's a cowboy so he took me up on it."

Kat forced a smile. "Well done, I'll love making it. Is it the cowboy at the corner table who requested it?"

"Yes. Even in this hot weather he's wearing a long-sleeved shirt."

Kat had noticed. "They get used to them to protect them from the sun and bugs while herding cattle all day.

From the wire while working fences, there are a lot of reasons a cowboy wears long sleeves. It's normal." She hadn't even thought about the shirt, just the look on his face when their gazes locked.

"His hat is in the seat next to him."

"I assumed that."

"I forget you're a cowgirl." Grinning Sean crossed his arms and leaned his hip against the counter, bringing him closer to her.

She took a step away, he was a really great waiter and a nice young man. Twenty-four to be exact and she liked him as a person but there was a distance she needed to keep with her employees, so after the step away, she turned toward her counter. "Thanks, now let's get to work."

Her thoughts on the cowboy, she started preparing his meal and pushed the attraction away, instead she focused on food—exactly what she needed to focus on. After all, this wasn't the first cowboy to come in and have a meal alone. They came in, at least to the bar area, usually with motives because it was well known that she was from the huge ranch.

Not just a ranch but one that expanded across the ocean to the coast of Texas. That made her a target and she knew it. But she was not an easy target as the last one had recently found out. He was no longer around.

Then there were those dudes who just dressed like a cowboy who came in thinking they might get a chance at love with her—but she was far from stupid and knew their mind was really on the land, oil, and her dad's attachment to her name. She'd grown used to it and though Sean was a fairly new waiter, he'd never seen this before, didn't know being a cowboy didn't give a customer special draw to her. She gave all her customers her best.

Sean had headed out but stopped at the water stand. "I'll let him know you're working on his meal when I take him this water refill. Cowboys can drink their water." He grinned when she looked at him, then he headed back through the door.

She almost laughed because it was true, cowboys knew how important water was and they drank a lot of it. This told her that a true cowboy was sitting out there by the water. It kept them from dehydrating while working cattle. Everyone needed it but a cowboy knew the importance of it out in the sun, working hard. This odd knowledge had her curiosity up because this made the cowboy at her dining table sound real.

She went to work preparing his meal as the other chefs worked on other orders. When it was finished, Sean came back in and carried it out. Unable to stop herself, she went to the swinging doors and looked out through the edge.

The cowboy was gazing out over the water when Sean set the plate before him. His handsome face instantly looked stunned by the dish, sliced steaks, propped on beautiful sliced potatoes, and sautéed pineapple slices. Then all drizzled with her wonderful Hawaiian topping—her special sauce that no one but her knew the ingredients.

She knew the instant he placed his fork in and took a bite of the steak that he liked it. The smile and the thumbs up to Sean gave it away.

A grinning Sean turned away as the cowboy placed his fork and knife on the plate and chewed slowly, enjoying the taste.

Kat's insides cheered as he actually savored what she'd created. Then to her surprise, he looked toward the door, caught her watching and he smiled—there was no denying the way her insides reacted with excitement.

She spun instantly to resist the attraction and went back to work.

Several minutes later Sean entered the kitchen. "He loves it. You got another winner, and Clay, the cowboy asked if he could meet you before he leaves. He wants to tell you his review in person. And I told him you always meet them if they ask."

"Thank you." It was true. She gave him time to finish then Kat smoothed her apron and sucked in a deep breath before heading out the door. The breeze whipped over her as she passed by the bar, saw the cowboy's gaze lock onto her, sending her pulse into erratic gymnastics. Like a true cowboy, he stood instantly, tall and in jeans and boots, his cowboy hat still resting in the empty chair. He had a lean but powerful build, wide shoulders, lean hips. Her gaze went to his strong jaw that led to brown hair blending with tanned skin. Tanned skin that clearly came from working out in the sun. He looked great—and why was her mind going there?

"Hello," she said, getting her thoughts in order. "I'm Kat McConnell, the owner, which I think you probably already know. Sean said you wanted to see me, said you enjoyed your meal," she rambled, totally off guard by the feel of his touch when he took her hand.

Completely electrified by his gentle but firm hand on hers.

* * *

Shock rammed through Clay as he took her hand. "It was amazing, really incredible. I'm Clay Samson," he forced out clearly. "The manager of your dad's ranch. He asked me to come meet you and enjoy your creations. And I'm glad I did."

The moment he'd taken her hand, her expression clouded slightly like his insides had at her touch—or was it the words he'd spoken that caused the clouds in her eyes? She stiffened up and dropped his hand.

"So, you're the new manager at my dad's ranch?" Obviously needing clarification on what he'd said, she studied him.

"Yes, your dad thought it would be good for us to meet. So, here I am, and glad I came, the food was the best I've ever had. I'd heard how well your restaurants did, and now I know why. You are an amazing chef."

Her eyes narrowed, clearly, he'd said something she didn't like. "Thanks. The meal is on me since you are the manager of my dad's ranch. I'll let him know you did as he asked."

Definitely something wrong. "And I'll tell him I've met you, the rancher's daughter who knows how to cook," he said it teasingly, hoping to ease the tension, but she stiffened.

"I'm not a rancher's kid when I'm in Kona. I'm a woman who loves deep-sea fishing and cooking dishes that make people enjoy their visit to my restaurant and the island."

"Sorry, I get it. Here in Kona, what many call the fishing capital of the world of King Fish fishing, I'm a cowboy, not a fisherman. Just a rancher who enjoys the view of the ocean from up on the mountain top there on your family ranch. I like the ranch, the view…" He halted his words, put a halter on them and changed his tone. "Anyway, I'll head out now. I'd fight you over the meal ticket, but I believe you are like your dad, not giving in when you get something on your mind. However," he said as he pulled a twenty dollar bill from his pocket and laid it on the table. "I'll pay Sean, he did a great job and if I come back, I'll be paying for my own meal."

"Fine, and again, I'll tell Dad you came by. And if you come back it's on you. Good night, Clay Samson."

"Good night, Kat McConnell—Chef Extraordinaire."

* * *

Heart pounding, hand tingling, Kat spun away. It sounded like the cowboy had come here at her dad's urging to meet her but not for any other reason. She was okay knowing her dad had pretty much obligated him to come down the mountain to meet her. That was a different reason than the last ranch manager had when he'd walked into her Café by the Seaside.

"You need to tell your dad to knock it off."

His quiet words reached her and she stopped in her tracks. She turned back. "What?"

The cowboy had stepped closer so his words were heard only by her. His expression serious, his bright green eyes dug deep. "I'm not here for any other reason than to do what your dad asked me to do. Us meeting sounded like a good idea since we do live on the same island and you are the boss's daughter. He probably wanted to make sure if you ever needed anything you knew you could call me and my cowboys. *But* if it bothers you, him sending me to do this, just tell him to stop. Or I'll tell him you don't need checking up on if he asks me to come again."

Startled, she actually liked his reaction. He hadn't come because he had heard she was single, like the previous guy. That man had also come to dinner one night but it was quite obvious he had come to see if there could be something between the two of them. To her relief nothing about that first meeting had been like this one. Thankfully there had been absolutely no attraction from her to the other cowboy—*unlike what you feel toward this one.*

Shoving those last words out of her mind she stepped closer to the Clay. "My dad's last hire left because he made a mistake with me."

"A mistake? Your dad didn't tell me why the spot was open."

"The job was vacated by the last man because he got a sudden job elsewhere after crossing a line with me."

They stared at each other, Clay's gaze darkened. "Crossing a line? A sudden job. So, what did he do to get this 'sudden' job?" The cowboy's jaw stiffened as he said the words, his eyes narrowed.

"He made unwanted passes at me." She didn't flinch from the deep look but took it as a good thing. It made Clay look like he wasn't looking for an easy target to romance like the last one. "The last manager thought if he could get Kat McConnell to fall for him, that he could be a part owner of the ranch. That wasn't and isn't happening."

She'd had a few words of warning to the cowboy fool that if he didn't resign, keeping their conversation between the two of them, that his inappropriate actions would have been made public and completely ruined his career in the horse and cattle industry. The McConnells were not to be messed with and she'd made it blatantly clear to the jerk that night. So clear that he'd resigned that next morning, mouth shut. Her dad, it seemed, had gotten a new, hopefully good man this time. One who now knew she was off limits.

Then, on the other hand, Clay had said her dad had asked him to come meet her—what was up with that?

CHAPTER THREE

Clay's insides churned with anger by the fact that the last manager hadn't just tried to date Kat, he'd basically wanted the ranch and wanted to use her to do that. "You did right. But your dad doesn't know what the jerk did?"

Her eyes narrowed. "No, and he won't."

It hit him then that she'd just thrown out a secret message between them. If her father found out, then she'd know he wasn't to be trusted. She obviously could handle it if her dad found out but this was her way of testing him.

He assumed Mitch would not like it and he wouldn't have either if he were a father—something he knew he would never be. "Got it. I'll head out and keep it your way. And who knows, you might see me again. Now, I can at least tell your dad I did what he asked me to do. You've got a great place here. Really great." Clay paused, turned back and she was still watching him. "Mitch told me that you used to like coming on the ranch when you were younger. But he said you never come out there anymore. Is there a reason for that, other than the fact that the last manager was a jerk?" Her eyes flickered telling him maybe there was some other reason she stayed away.

"I love the life I've built. But… I might come back out there at some point. There's just not really been a reason to," she said, her words drifting.

Something didn't seem right. "If you ever need to come out, please do. I'll stay out of your way or I'll show you around, it would be your choice. The ranch has changed some since I've been there. I've been working on some updates. But, you might just want a quiet ride alone to that hill that overlooks the ocean. It's amazing and not quite as high as looking down from an airplane as you fly over heading to Texas or back to

Kona. But it's perfect serenity from that spot with the bench." Why had he said that he wasn't sure but he found the spot perfect and from the look on her face he'd said something that triggered her eyes to suddenly look slightly sad.

"I loved that view, actually my favorite spot is sitting on that bench." She clasped her hands, released them and placed one on her hip, her head tilting as her thoughts obviously went into action. "You're right. I might have to surprise my dad and come out to the ranch. Take a ride up there on that mountainside."

His chest tightened. "Your dad would like that."

"He'd be shocked. My friend and I used to go up there with my sisters when we were teenagers. She just came with us a few times but the last time it was just the two of us up there on that mountainside."

Her voice drifted off with those words and her amazing gaze grew misty. Clay knew something was wrong but it wasn't his place to push. "Come on any time. It's a beautiful place you obviously are connected with."

She gave a small smile. "All right."

He nodded. "See you later." And then he turned and walked away determined not to look back over his shoulder.

He knew now without doubt that there was a reason that his boss, his friend, had sent him here. Mitch was no dummy. That man knew ranching, cattle, and people. That's why his business was so huge. That's why his ranching ability was so fantastic. And, basically, he knew that Clay knew his business too.

He also knew Clay didn't need the money he made managing this ranch, he needed the open mountainside overlooking the water. Needed to work to help him get through life because sitting wasn't something his heart needed after what life had dealt him. Mitch McConnell had hired him more to help heal Clay's hurting heart. Mitch might be a quiet man, but he had eyes that dug deep.

Obviously, those eyes saw something in his strong, tough daughter Kat that needed more than she'd found so far.

What did Kat need? She was, as his friend called her, the strong one. But it was clear he saw she needed something… and it clearly had something to do with that spot on the hillside.

That spot that Clay found peace at. Most of the time.

Mitch was obviously a mind and heart reader… but what spot in that did Clay hold? Hopefully, his boss wasn't making the mistake of thinking he was a matchmaker.

Clay wasn't looking and clearly neither was Kat. But the friend she was talking about was, if he was right, her brother's first wife, the first one who died. He thought about that as he walked down the street, he'd seen sorrow in her eyes. Sorrow he could understand. That hillside was where he could release his sorrow… was that what Kat's father thought she needed?

He reached his truck and climbed inside. Started the engine and pulled out, then headed toward the mountain.

Since losing his wife, he had purposely stayed away from dating again. He wanted nothing to do with taking a chance on ever having a hurting heart again.

He had no plans to ever take the chance on loving again and losing.

No, he focused on the beauty surrounding him here on the island, it was stunning, and for him it was the quiet life he needed. But it was lonely… and as he drove up the mountain, that loneliness suddenly grabbed hold and held on.

* * *

The golden rays of sun barely peeked softly over the horizon above the volcano as Kat strode past the huge number of fishing boats of all sizes. They were all waiting to be taken out onto the stunning blue waters off the coast of her favorite place, this wonderful Island of Hawai'i, and her town, Kona.

Here the waters dropped deep almost instantly and the volcanos protected the waters on Kona's side making them calm almost always—perfect for fishing. But for her, more important, exactly why she was taking her boat out at this very early hour—on these waters she found peace when she needed it. And this morning she needed the calm waters to work their magic. She'd been rattled after meeting the new manager of their family's ranch. So rattled that she hadn't slept, thinking about him and doing as he suggested—visiting the ranch.

She needed to be on the incredibly calm bay that set the view from Kona apart from most waters known for fishing. This hour in the morning to Kat, was her heart-touching time of the day, not the huge fish, the Blue Marlin, that made it so startlingly wonderful and called to her often. This morning it was the serene waters of her special place along the shore where she was forced to feel peace when she so desperately needed it.

No one looking at her would realize that peace was a struggle for her that she had to force on herself sometimes. She was known for strength through and through and no one, not even her sisters, knew that sometimes she felt far weaker than she showed the world. Or her family.

This was one of those mornings.

Just four days ago she'd flown nearly nine hours across the ocean from the wedding of her beautiful sister Pearl. And not too long ago her sister Dora had also married and was now living a beautiful life. Her brother, who'd lost his wife, Olivia, their best friend, had also found love again. For all of them, Kat was happy and knew that Oliva would be or was too, looking down from above.

But Kat had no intention of opening her heart to anyone. She couldn't deny that the cowboy from last night had tugged at something she'd never felt before inside of her. She was strong for everyone, felt joy for them and had so enjoyed the celebrations. But she'd fought off the thoughts since flying home, thoughts that had plagued her since giving her family hugs before she'd climbed onto the plane and flown back to Kona.

She'd fought off the unease and been working instead of stepping onto her boat, but after last night's meeting with Clay, she'd needed the peace waiting for her out there on the water at this early hour where no one was watching her. Here was her escape from expectations. Kona was her safe haven, especially when driving her boat out to the open space of the blue waters and the coastline that she loved.

Her boat, a simple twenty-four-foot fishing boat, white with a teal stripe running along its edge, was her haven. Wasting no time, she quickly checked everything, turned the key and let the engine roar to life, sending an instant smile to her face and ease through her spirit.

She unwrapped the ropes from the dock then returned to the wheel and drove carefully past the professional fishing boats as their crews prepared them for the day. Their clients would be arriving within the next hour or two and the crews had grown accustomed to seeing her head out alone this early many mornings of the year before everyone else. When she wanted to fish for a huge Blue Marlin, which she couldn't do alone, she hired one of these teams to take her on her adventure.

But all other times she took her own boat out alone.

As she reached the narrow-jutted edge leaving the ocean endless in front of her, she turned her boat left instead of heading out; she headed down the shoreline. The endless black lava rock and sweeping water calling her as the waves rolled in, hit the lava rocks that were sculpted with holes and cavities that filled instantly, and she watched as the waters from the lava cavities then exploded with powerful beauty up into the air. Sending massive sprays of the blue water and white foam up toward the sky, toward heaven and rising pink and gold light from the rising sun.

Watching, speechless as always, this was the coastline she loved, the coast that took her internal anger churning hard and tough through her now and like the waves now spewing upward she felt relief too. As the beautiful rising sun turned the foam and water of the bay and released it upward, it did the same for her anger that she held in for no one to see. Here, as if she'd thrown her troubling emotions into the rocks, the rocks took them then blew them up through its lava holes toward heaven, and she slowly felt the internal peace ease in over her that she needed.

Who would know that watching her family rejoice with happiness and ease would cause all this pent-up stress inside of her? But it did and she'd handled it until the cowboy stepped in last night and reminded her that she had something waiting for her at the ranch... something Olivia had told her she'd left for her there.

Seeing her family living with joy and happiness was a great thing, yet tension that she held in and showed no one, raged through her now. But standing here at the wheel of her boat, slowly driving the coast the strain eased with each blast of the waters on the rocks.

No one knew how hard it was for her to watch their happiness. No one knew she feared losing one of them or watching one of them lose the love of their lives like she'd watched her brother lose his sweet Olivia. Finding love like they had and losing it was not something she was going to take a chance on.

The shining specks blasting upward in the sun was her release, but also reminded her that life was hers to choose.

And she chose this, chose to live alone with only God and His creation to know her heart and hear her pain. The pain she felt after seeing her family's joy and knowing she would never see that for herself.

She just couldn't risk it. She closed her eyes as the old song *When Peace Like A River* flowed through her. Olivia's song, a reminder that her sweet friend wanted them all to find peace. In their own way. But for Kat, the lyrics that came in the song and the Bible, were that it was well with her soul. She found peace like a river, or for her peace on the ocean here at Kona. It was still hard at times to accept but here God gave her some peace on these gentle waters. But last night without knowing it she'd been reminded by the cowboy that once she'd wanted a happily-ever-after.

No more though. She would never let herself chance it. Here on the waters of Kona she found the strength to keep her mind on her work.

No matter what more her family hoped for her. Or… that the cowboy reminded her of what she'd never have, and the man had no idea what he'd done.

On top of that he'd also invited her to her ranch and in his eyes when he'd asked her to come, the words coming out of nowhere to slam into her and still gripped as she turned the boat back toward the marina.

It was time to get back to work. Cooking and testing new creations on customers was where her joy was and that was the way she would keep it.

Maybe while working today she'd figure out her next step—was she going to go to the ranch?

CHAPTER FOUR

Three days had passed since Kat met the new man overseeing their ranch. Two mornings since she'd taken her sunrise boat ride to help with her troubled thoughts he'd stirred up inside of her.

Thoughts that were still on her mind about the ranch she hadn't been out to for a long time.

She spent time cooking in the afternoons and evenings at the restaurant, staying busy as usual but each time the door to the kitchen opened and she glimpsed the table in the corner she visualized Clay sitting there at the water's edge. Something inside of her wished he would come back. Why?

The small moment in time that they'd talked dug

deep inside of her for some reason. Was it his quietness, his general way of speaking to her, the captivating way he looked at her—as if he could see through her? Because it *was* as if he did see through her.

He saw, like no one else had ever seen except maybe her dad, that she missed something about the ranch. Her dad had obviously realized that and sent him to invite her. She loved her restaurants, but her ranching had once been something special in her life that she enjoyed too but she'd purposefully pushed it away.

Her thought went back to that hillside, the one Clay had talked about. The place where she and Olivia had sat on Olivia's last visit to the Kona ranch. On that hillside overlooking the blue waters, the beautiful horizon of other islands and their volcanoes in the distance, sitting on that mountainside she and Olivia had talked.

A few years later, before Olivia died, her sweet friend told her she'd left her something there buried beneath that bench. But It had been almost five years since losing her friend and Kat hadn't been back to that bench. Hadn't searched for what Olivia had left her.

She closed her eyes, now finished with slicing the steak, thoughts whirled in her brain, she had tried so hard to ignore the last moment Olivia spoke to her. When she'd held her hand, pulled her close, and whispered, "Go back to *our* spot. I buried something for you there." Those had been her dear friend's last barely whispered words to her. Yet, she had *not* gone back.

What would Olivia have buried there for her? And why hadn't she been able to go find out?

She could no longer use the manager who'd made the maddening pass at her as an excuse. He was gone. And no longer an excuse.

She looked over her shoulder and motioned to the waiting waiter that the dish was ready. Her hands on her hips, she stepped back as he picked up the plate and headed out the door to deliver it to the one who ordered it. Kat's gaze followed him out the door and landed on the table by the sea... As the door swung closed her thoughts were on the cowboy who'd invited her to come to the ranch.

It was time.

She felt Olivia rooting her on from heaven and

knew it was time to go dig up the past.

She'd removed her apron with those thoughts rolling through her mind, and now she walked over to Chef Ridge, her main chef. "I'll be leaving now. Y'all do a great job and I'm grateful for each of you. See you later."

The small, older man smiled. "Whatever's calling you out tonight it's a great thing. You spend too much time in this kitchen when you're on the island."

"You're right." She winked at him then headed out, reaching for her purse as she passed her office that she shared with him. Outside she slipped into her Jeep and within moments, she calmly eased out of the parking space and onto the road of the moonlit night.

Passing through town, music from the restaurants along the street surrounding her, she stopped at the stop sign, then she turned right and headed to the roads that would carry her home. Only then did she realize that she wasn't heading to her apartment, which was one further down the road she'd taken. No, on this road she was heading toward the countryside, the ranch that used to be home.

At the next stop sign she headed decisively toward her apartment. It was nighttime. Not the time to startle Clay with her arrival. What was she thinking? When she reached home, she pulled into her small garage, pushed the button, and the door came down.

Inside, she dropped her purse off on the side table, then walked out onto her deck where she sank down into the cushions of her chair. She gazed out at the moon shining on the water as her thoughts reeled. Everything seemed to be colliding inside her head and heart.

Less than a week ago, after her sister Pearl's wedding, she'd arrived back here on her island, but things from her Texas home on Star Gazer Island had followed her. Yes, her brother and her sisters were all married now and so very happy.

She opened her eyes and caught the falling star over the water as it sped through the sky, no limits on it as it disappeared out of view.

That had been sweet Olivia. Her friend, who had known she was dying, yet lived life with a smile.

Kat was the woman, the kid, the one who always confronted problems before everyone else. She was a protector who hadn't been able to protect her friend. But her sweet friend had known she was the control freak, had known that not being able to control keeping her alive would always weigh heavy on her heart.

Losing Olivia had been the hardest time of her life and she knew she'd never risk falling in love because that could be even worse, and she wasn't going there. But lately, since watching her family find love, her heart was acting up. The strict order she lived by was getting disorderly.

Her dad was concerned enough about her to send Clay to meet her. That meant she wasn't doing a good job of hiding everything she tried to hide and keep to herself. Her dad, who knew how strong she was, knew that she was a protector. But he was obviously a watchman and knew it was time to let her know he was watching whether she wanted him to be or not.

She'd deal with that when she saw him but aside from his intervening in her life, she knew right now the main thing was time to confront whatever Olivia had left for her.

Sitting there in the darkness with the moon shining

over the water, she knew it was time to confront a memory and do what Olivia had asked her to do. Go back to the mountain.

She stood up, walked inside, closed the door and locked it, pulled the drape closed then headed to her bedroom. In the morning, she had a mission.

* * *

Clay was gearing up for a ride on his day off. His saddle bags with his lunch inside were in place as he readied himself for his ride. It was his day off and going to be a good day.

Not that he normally went anywhere on his day off other than out riding alone for the enjoyment of being in the saddle, rather than rounding up cattle and working. But today was a celebration day.

Today was the day his life had changed in a dramatic, unwanted way that he'd learned to live with. Now, on his wife's death date, he celebrated that she was safe in the hands of the Lord, and not just lost in the deep waters of the ocean that had taken her from him.

It had taken him some time to get to this point, but he knew this was how she would want him to take her death. And so, he'd made the commitment to look at her death in a different way. As she often said, "We each have our time on earth and the rest is up to us." She'd say it with a smile, her beautiful heart touching smile. "The day I die I'll be in heaven so no worrying about me. Be happy, live life fully… God is so good." The day she'd made that statement to him they'd been on a boat and she'd looked up to heaven then closed her eyes smiling. And he, like the love-struck cowboy he'd been had looked at her… not up at the heavens she loved.

Now, her words ringing in his ears, his heart solid in knowing he too knew the Lord because of her, and was thankful for that. What he hadn't done so far was live life fully, like she wished for him. He still mourned, in a more distant way the life he'd lost, the life he'd momentarily been blessed to know.

But no matter what he knew he would never think about risking loving and losing like that again. He couldn't, wouldn't take the risk of losing like that again. Besides that not everyone knew love like that in their life once, much less taking the chance on knowing it twice.

He lifted his boot and placed it in the stirrup just as the sound of an engine rose through the warm air. Looking over his shoulder he saw the red Jeep driving up the long, curved, white rock road of the ranch. The top was off the Jeep and he saw wind whipping the curling auburn red hair of the driver. His pulse kicked in seeing Kat as she rounded the last curve, crossed the cattle guard of ranch property with no hesitation. It was clear that she knew where every curve and twist was as she drove up the hillside and across the rough cattle guard.

His heart rattled inside his chest like it had the night when their gazes locked at her restaurant. His reaction didn't please him, then or now.

Unlike him, she was smiling big as she pulled to a halt. He kicked himself mentally, he had invited her and it was her ranch. He strode her way as she hopped from the Jeep. Tall, lean, with her wild red hair, the woman was stunning whether he wanted to acknowledge it or not.

"Good morning," he said. "I'm guessing by that smile that you're not here to tell me I shouldn't have come to town."

Hands on lean hips she held his gaze. "No. I'm here to thank you for coming to town. And to thank you for reminding me that I should come out here and do what I've been needing to do, no more putting it off. So, if you don't mind, I'd like to saddle a horse and head up the hill."

Stunned, he smiled back at the now serious expression of the lady. "I'd be glad to saddle a horse for you or, *your* horse if you show me which one it is. I was actually heading up to the overlook myself. But if you want to go alone I'll hang back. If you don't mind a riding partner we can go together. It's my day off so nothing's holding me back."

Her eyes brightened. "You're off and hanging out at the ranch and riding up the hill?"

"Yes." He smiled, couldn't help it. "It is a beautiful ranch and though I work it every day riding for peace of mind and enjoyment time is what I do on my day off. And well, it's special there on the hill as you also know."

"Yes, it is, but you can see it any time, still, you go there instead of taking a real day off?"

"Your dad tells me to take a day off all the time whenever I need it, but I don't often."

She studied him. "That tells me there's a reason that you're taking today off and going to that hillside."

The woman knew things. "Yes. Like you, I like it there, sitting and watching the waves and the boats. On my day off I don't have to worry about what time I need to come home or wonder what cattle I have to go catch and work on."

Gazes locked, his heart suddenly raged like a wild bull busting from a closed pen. He forced his focus on business, "I'll go saddle a horse. Do you have a favorite?"

She smiled that amazing smile then walked past him toward the horse stable. "Ladybug is mine. I broke her, trained her, love her, and hope she's doing good. She's probably going to be mad at me."

He grinned as he caught up to her. "So *that's* what her problem is. Ladybug has not been the best, ever since I got here, and they all told me that she's been like that for a while now. So, you left her to deal with you not being here all by herself?"

Kat stopped at the wide entrance, her gaze dimming as she met his. "Yes. I guess I did, and I'm sorry. I hope she'll forgive me."

Caught by the real look of regret on her face he regretted his words. "I have a feeling her ears are going to perk up, her tail will swish, and she's going to be excited the moment she sees you. She's in the last stall."

She smiled and with determined steps headed down the walkway. He hesitated for a moment watching her, she wore jeans on her lean legs, cowboy boots, and a soft tan shirt that went well with her hair. But it was the alert looks of the horses in the stalls, their eyes dancing and their ears all perked up as they held their heads out over their gates watching her move past them. They all gave welcoming whinnies as they nodded their heads. They knew and remembered her. Then, from the last stall, Ladybug's chestnut-toned head popped over the gate, her large hazelnut eyes locked on the lady—that had the same tones of hair and eyes as the spunky horse. The horse that obviously had been sad as now Clay saw a jolt of excitement and recognition instantly. Excitement popped into the horse's eyes and the wild, fierce whinny that erupted from the old horse told the story. This was who she loved. Who she'd been missing.

Clay was stunned, this was a quiet horse. Now he knew it had been a lost horse, a hurting horse. A mourning horse.

"Hey there, Ladybug. I'm back," Kat said softly. Ladybug now let out a soft nicker, lifted her head, flopped her tail from side to side, then the old horse rested her jaw on Kat's shoulder. Kat's arms went around Ladybug's neck and she buried her face in the horse's cinnamon mane.

Clay witnessed the touching reunion as it happened and immediately wondered why Kat left behind an animal that obviously loved her dearly.

CHAPTER FIVE

"It's been a while since you've seen this horse."

Clay's words rattled through Kat as she nodded against her beloved horse's mane. "Yes. I guess this proves that." She looked at the cowboy, seeing compassion in his eyes.

"An animal loves forever."

"I love her too," her voice broke. "Life just got me off course." She leaned back and smiled at Ladybug. "You ready for a ride?" The horse whinnied and nodded as if it understood. Kat laughed and hugged the horse again.

"Does this have to do with losing your sister-in-law?"

His quiet question hit home. "Yes, my sweet friend Olivia wanted me and my sisters to live life to its fullest. And I do that with my cooking and my restaurants." She paused her mind on Olivia. "I was so blessed to know her."

"She was an awesome person, it sounds like."

"Amazing."

"And, obviously, left a great legacy behind."

Kat's heart clenched and she locked eyes with him. "Absolutely. But I've not been doing what her last request to me was." She halted her words, opened the stall, walked inside, found the bridle hanging where it always was, right outside the gate. She took it in with her, caressed the horse's neck, ran her hand across its back and thigh in calming moves, talking gently to the horse the whole time. "Ladybug, you're looking great."

Clay leaned against the stall gate watching her. She could see him out of the corner of her eye but was afraid to look at him. She'd almost let him see her weakness. Weakness didn't sound right, though oddly weakness was the strength that drove her.

Olivia had recognized it early, even before she was going to die she'd known that Kat wasn't as strong as she pretended to be. Now, she focused on getting the harness and bridle on the horse, then led her outside to where Clay was now waiting with a saddle in his hands.

"Is this the right one? It has your initials on it, I believe."

"You're observant. Yes. It's mine."

He placed the saddle onto the saddle blanket that he had held in one hand and slipped it onto Ladybug's back like a professional, knowing what he was doing. And then the saddle was hoisted with one arm and his hip, he gently placed it on Ladybug and within seconds he'd reached beneath the horse and secured the saddle in place.

The cowboy knew exactly what he was doing. What he didn't know, she hoped, was how watching him moments ago and seeing emotion in his face, his expression moved crates of emotions around inside her chest.

"If you're ready, let's hit the trail. I have lunch. I have plenty in case you're worried about eating."

She smiled, even laughed, which gave her emotions a little relief. "Well, just so you know, I have a saddle bag with me, and it too is packed with a few goodies."

"Alright then. I think we're going to be just fine." He'd walked out into the sunshine, and she followed him, leading Ladybug. The man had a determined stride that meant he knew where he was going and what he was doing. She admired him—that ability, agility.

Okay, she gave in and admitted that the man was stunning and amazingly good-looking. And thankfully a bit distracting from the turmoil that going up the mountain to see what Olivia had left filled her with inside. She needed that.

The thing that seemed to pull her the most was he gave her space even though she saw sympathy or knowledge or something in his gaze. He was so far a perfect cowboy, showing his strength through quietness.

He handed her the reins, their fingers touched—lightning vaulted through her and she almost jumped back she was so stunned. Crazy awareness wrapped around her like nothing she'd ever felt before.

Clay stepped back, his gaze held hers for just a

slight instant as if he'd felt it too. How could he not have it was so blunt?

But, he turned and stalked—yes, *stalked* to his horse, unhooked it from the arena fence, and in one swift, beautiful motion, he was in the saddle.

Amazing.

"You going to saddle up?"

She realized she was still standing there staring. Taking a wakeup breath she took two strides, her boot in the stirrup, and instantly swung her right leg over then slid into the seat, both boots in their stirrup. It had been a while and she was a bit shook up, so thankfully she hadn't missed the stirrup and landed face-first on the ground.

She looked at the cowboy, who was now looking at her. "Good job."

Taking a breath and feeling more confident she said, "My dad taught me early on, that once a cowgirl or boy always. Obviously, it's true."

He smiled. "It's true. Let's head out."

"Hold on, I forgot to get my saddlebags." She rode the horse over to her Jeep, hopped from the back of

Ladybug, then pulled her beautiful leather saddlebag out of the back of the Jeep. Quickly, she strapped it to the back of the saddle then she settled back in the saddle. "Okay. Now I'm ready."

"Then here we go." They headed toward the main fence line that led onto the ranch. He leaned down and opened the gate without getting off his horse and let her pass by him.

Suddenly as she rode past Clay into the open land she felt a gush of freedom as she surveyed the rolling landscape. Landscape that once they reached the top would give her the magnificent view she loved of both land and ocean.

This had once been her happy place. But right now, she focused on her reason for being here. The mystery of sweet Olivia's hidden treasure, a treasure she was sure came straight from Olivia's heart.

It had been waiting all this time and today she would finally do as she should have already done. Dig it up and let her friend touch her heart one more time.

Why had she put it off for so long?

WHAT'S FOREVER GOT TO DO WITH IT

* * *

Clay closed the gate, sat straight in the saddle then slowly followed Kat. He felt he needed to give her some space to take in the beauty of the land before her that she hadn't seen or ridden on for a very long time.

He also knew from his own experiences that she might need a moment alone—she'd looked sad as she passed him heading onto the land so he gave her space.

Honestly, he hadn't thought she would show up, but here she was leading the way to his quiet spot. Which had been, he now knew, her spot first.

The beautiful woman riding ahead of him leading the way had no idea that she was going to *his* Saturday afternoon spot.

Sitting there overlooking that ocean was this cowboy's place. And now he knew that it had also been Kat's place. He couldn't help but wonder what was hidden there on the beautiful hillside. Some called it a mountain, some a hilltop, some a volcano, but he called it his place of peace.

He hoped she could find peace also because

something was bothering her. He'd felt it that night at the restaurant but he felt it even stronger today. Of course, she was here looking for what Olivia had left her, that probably explained everything. He too was curious and he hoped he could help her find what had been left for her.

She looked over her shoulder meeting his gaze, and once again he pushed away the thoughts of attraction. Yes, he was attracted, but that was as far as it was going to go. He had loved and lost, and he would never go there again.

"It's as beautiful as I always remembered," Kat called, then waved her hand telling him to catch up.

One tiny touch of his spur and his horse quickened his steps and put Clay riding comfortably beside Kat.

Comfortably. The word had just come out of nowhere but as he smiled at her there was a comfort he found beside her. Also, a protective feeling and he was glad she'd let him come with her—only because he could tell she seemed a little stressed out.

Not knowing what her friend had left her was probably what was wrong. Yeah. That would be a mystery, a hard to understand mystery maybe. "It's a great ride," he said. "I enjoy it every time I make it. Not many people get to ride up a hillside this grassy, steep, and beautiful. Especially knowing on the other side is going to be another downhill slope."

"Right, a downhill slope that looks as if it ends at the ocean, though we know it doesn't. It ends at flatter land that leads to a road, not the ocean."

"I haven't seen it from that view."

"I forgot you haven't been out on the water. So, from the water in this particular section it just looks like a hill then it's cut off leaving the people from the boats thinking it's the ending." She looked thoughtful as he took in her words. "You know, that makes me think about life. Sometimes we think our life is on an uphill escalating peak, and then we'll know that it has ups and downs, hardships and happy times that happen in the middle road that cuts through life like it does over that hill."

He studied the beautiful woman, her expression was so serious, and her words cut deep. Very deep. "Exactly," he said. "Do you find yourself on that middle road?" Their gazes met as their horses' steps slowed, as if in step with their thoughts.

"I am right now, actually," she said. "It's shocking in a way. I have a great life. I'm alive. You know? And I know the Lord. I know that's the most important thing in my life and that came from Olivia. She led me to the Lord, told me one day we'd meet again, if I too accepted the Lord into my heart."

Her words struck him hard, sounding just like his wife's words.

"She said that to me here on this hillside. That was one of the many things we talked about. So, I know one day I'll see her again."

Her words touched a chord inside of him.

"What about you?" she asked. "How do you understand that?"

Only then did he realize he'd been nodding when she looked at him. He slightly hitched his shoulder. "When you are the one left behind, you feel lost in the middle. I lost my wife." They'd reached the top of the mountain and he looked below and let his gaze drift out over the beautiful sea. "One day I'll see her again too."

"I'm so sorry. I had no idea you lost your wife. How long ago?"

"Four years today," he said, pushing the words out. "She was a great fisherman. Me, I'm a cowboy. She was a champion at deep-sea fishing. Like you like to do. Honestly, I think that's why your dad thought we should meet."

Her expression softened. "You're probably right. He knows you know a thing or two about deep-sea fishing because of your wife."

"Believe me, I'm not a fisherman. I am a cowboy. But Natalie was an amazing fisherman. I was managing a ranch in Florida when we met. Most people only think about Florida with beaches and don't realize there are some beautiful ranches there too. Great horses too. That's how I met your dad. We were in the Florida Keys at Marathon and Natalie was fishing in a major offshore fishing tournament, and your dad and mom were there. Me and Natalie were eating at the restaurant's bar as it was too packed to get a table. Your parents ended up sitting at the bar beside of us for dinner. We got into a great conversation."

"That's understandable, my Dad can talk cattle, horses, and fishing anywhere."

"Yes, he can. He loved the idea that I was a cowboy married to a fisherwoman." He chuckled, "As he called her." He paused then, where was he going with this story? "I guess if we're being truthful, your dad knew I needed a change when he hired me because he'd met me with Natalie alive and well. He also told us that he had a daughter who was a restaurant owner, a great cook, and had just lost her best friend. He was worried about you." He paused remembering that moment.

"At that moment Natalie, there in front of your mom and dad, took my hand and looked at your dad and told him she was so sorry for all of you. She said she understood that when you married, that meant one day one of you would lose your best friend. Then she looked me in the eyes and said she hoped she wasn't the one that ever had to live through that. Then she squeezed my hand hard." His heart pounded hard at the memory, Natalie had leaned in and kissed him gently, then smiled. "This cowboy is the strong one."

He wasn't as strong as she'd assumed.

Kat reached out from her seat in the saddle and squeezed his arm. "That must be the connection, Natalie made a mark on Dad's heart."

"I always remember that moment, and your dad and mom do too. It wasn't during the tournament but three days later that she died."

"I'm so sorry. What happened?"

"We went out on a boat together. Not to fish but to relax after she'd won first prize. We went out to relax out at the hump. I'm sure you know where that is."

Kat nodded. "I know that spot well between USA and Cuba. Deep water, just not as deep as Kona's water but a lot of miles further offshore and where fishermen loved to fish. What happened?"

"It was a beautiful day. Then while we were out there, suddenly a terrible storm blew in almost out of nowhere, and we started back. The waters were rough. She was driving the boat, she loved driving when she wasn't fishing. I was beside her. It turned into a monster storm. The waves were larger than I'd ever seen. And then a huge wave rolled in—we, the boat went up in the air, came down hard and threw me to one side and threw

Natalie over the side before I could grab her. The water was dark and deep and I cut the engine but... I couldn't find her in the water. I searched. And searched, and called for help. I clutched a life float ready to throw it if I saw her. And ready to dive in when I found her. And then I saw her arm wave from way off in the distance."

His heart roared and hurt as he told the story he hated. "Sorry, I didn't mean to go there."

Her hand tightened on his arm. "Please finish telling me."

"We never found her. I dove in and fought the waves trying to get to her, to find her, until they pulled me out. They could have left me in, I couldn't save her. She was gone."

* * *

"I'm so sorry." Kat gently touched his arm, felt the tension there and her heart ached for him. "I can't even imagine. You know what my brother lived through. You've lived it."

"We all know when we marry someone, we could lose them. I learned it quicker than I wanted."

She pulled her hand away. "I'll never marry, no matter what. My family, all of them are now telling me that love lives on."

"That's true."

She started riding down the hill toward the bench. He rode beside her and she looked at him. "I am so sorry. My dad knew that you becoming a rancher here on Kona would get you away from the coast there in America. I mean, this is America, but here you're at a distance. You've got ranchland with a view. Maybe they thought it would give you some distance and healing from way up here."

"Your dad obviously sees things. He remembered Natalie's words in the restaurant that night. He checked on me several times and knew that I left my job in Florida and then moved to, of all places, Montana. The ranch land with no view of the ocean. He knew that I still struggled. And then he called me and offered me this job. He told me I would have the ranch land, but when I needed it, I could also have the view of the ocean. And if I ever decided I wanted to go out there on the water again, it would be waiting for me."

Kat was stunned by her father's words, his thoughts. The man might not always be the biggest talker in the world, but, obviously, he watched, listened, and acted. She loved her dad more in that moment than ever before and she already loved him as much as she'd thought possible.

"This is a perfect place," Clay said. "Ranchland, cattle, horses, beaches, and the best fishing for Blue Marlin that there is, so I've been told. But right here it's the best view of all of it and he knew it. I'm glad we came."

"I am too," she said, and she was. Clay was overcoming more than she was and seeing his pain made her more certain than before that she would never marry and have to face loss like his.

She could see the love of his for his wife in his eyes, hear it in his words, saw it in the movement of his hands on the reins that gripped the saddle horn as he looked out over the water.

Her eyes stayed pinned to him. "So I guess now that we are on these terms, we'll search for a treasure. Olivia has left me a treasure hunt, and I think my father thought maybe you might need a treasure hunt too."

He looked at her then a slow smile lifted and she clearly knew one of the reasons his wife had loved him. His deep-sea fishing wife had to have loved his smile.

Kat nodded. "Let's ride." And with that, they each nudged their horse and rode the rest of the way down the hillside to the wooden bench that gave anyone sitting on it the most beautiful view of the topaz blue waters of the ocean and the cerulean skies above.

CHAPTER SIX

Clay no longer had any doubt that Mitch had a reason for sending him to Kat's restaurant that night. And he was okay with that because he now understood that he could help her find what she was here to find. But he also wanted to be here with her when they found whatever Olivia had left her. He understood and felt his sweet wife's hand on his shoulder, knowing she was pleased.

They tied their horses to a branch of a Sandalwood tree several feet away from the bench then they took their saddlebags and walked over to the bench.

"Now what?" Clay studied the ground beneath the bench as Kat sat down on it, setting her bag at her feet.

"It's been a long time since I sat here. I'm in my spot and Olivia sat right there." She patted the spot beside her. "I just can't figure out when she would have hidden something here."

The bench was long and had plenty of room for them. She had patted the place on the left as Olivia's seat so he sat down on the right of her and placed his bag beside hers.

"It's a great view," she said, studying the beautiful water.

"It's why I come and sit here at least once or twice a month. There's peace looking out over the water. Natalie would have loved it out there. And at first that was the main reason I came up here, to look at what she would have loved, but then it became my peaceful place."

"I'm betting she would like that. Like that you found a peaceful place."

"Yes, she would." He looked around. "So, the last time you and Olivia sat on this bench, what age were you?"

"We'd graduated." She paused. "It seems like a

long time ago, since I'm thirty-two now. We had no idea at that time she would be diagnosed a few years later with cancer. We were just young and dreaming. She was a true deep thinker, she dug in asking questions and she listened. And she *always* thought of others first."

"It's hard to lose people you love. But Kat, we both learned we have to take what life gives us—there is no choice.

"No, there are choices, life just changes them sometimes." Kat's eyes dug deep.

"Right." And she was.

"She loved being friends with all of us; me and my sisters. At that time, none of us girls had any idea she loved my brother. I mean, my sweet, strong brother. He thought she was just his friend, one of his younger sisters. Until he found out she was dying and he realized what he was losing. Only then, did we all realize how much she'd loved him from afar. And we hadn't even seen it."

Her words touched his heart. "She sounds really sweet."

"She was. That day we were sitting here, we talked

about families. Kids and seeing them running here on this land. Our kids playing together. I had no idea in her mind she was thinking of kids with my brother."

"You were young and thinking of your kids playing here." He liked the soft look that came to her eyes.

"Yes, but I also wanted to have my business. I love the ranch but needed space. I wanted my own life, not just my life that I was born into. A lot of people don't understand that, think I'm selfish because I had a wonderful life growing up. We talked about that I think that day."

"When do you think she left, whatever it is, here?"

"The day after we talked sitting here, I had to go help with the roundup. She stayed at the house and I've thought about it and think she might have taken the four-wheeler and come back up here."

"I don't always ride the horse up here. There are several four-wheelers for use. I can see how she could have gotten up here and back without you realizing she had done it. But I wonder why?"

"Me too. It must have been something that she really felt strongly about. It has sat here in the same spot all these years?"

He stood up. "Are you ready to find it?"

"I am. Let's do this."

"Did you bring something in that large saddle bag of yours?" It was a larger bag.

"I did. I brought a foldable camping shovel. I don't think she would have needed to bury whatever it is deep. And we have these in the supply barn, so that or ones like this would have been easy to carry. We used them when we were herding the cattle across the land and spent the night under the stars."

"I bet you're right. And I bet that was a great experience lying here at night looking at this view in the moonlight."

She reached for her bag and pulled it over to where she sat, opened it, then pulled the shovel out. "It was one of my favorite times growing up. I might have to do that again one day."

"You've got me wanting to do it now." They smiled at each other.

"You'd like it. Okay, so I think she probably buried it near the base, near the legs. We're sitting on dirt that's on hard lava rock in many places so it might take a few digs."

"You know your land. Do you want me to dig or do you want to dig?" She handed him the shovel.

"Please dig."

He took the shovel, his hand brushing hers as he took it, sending an electric vibe through him. "I think the best place to start is right there beneath where she sat because it's from her and you knew exactly where you each sat."

"Yes, I think you're right. Or, maybe under mine. Let's find out."

He knelt down. She hadn't moved and now on one knee they were looking at each other. He had a sudden want to cup her face with his palm, give her a little comfort as he saw stress in those determined eyes of her. The woman had a strong spirit. He could tell. She didn't like feeling weak.

He understood that. He didn't like it either.

"I better get out of the way," she said, then knelt beside him.

He smiled at her. "Let's do this." And then he started digging. Only about six inches down he heard metal meet metal. He looked at Kat. "I think I just heard metal."

"Me too," she said.

Within a few minutes, he'd dug up a rusting small metal container. It was actually a lunchbox. He dusted it off and the smiling happy faced heart appeared. Kat gasped then smiled.

"That would be her," Kat said as she took the box in her hand. "This was mine and she thought it was so cute. I forgot about it but she didn't. I told her the eyes on the heart looked like hers, the girl with the big heart." Her voice trembled. "That's what she had."

Clay stood up. "I'm going to go stand over there and give you this time alone."

She shifted from kneeling to sitting on the bench. "Thank you."

He walked over to the edge of the hill and looked out at the deep waters. His mind was full, thinking of his wife, seeing her beautiful smile, then he felt her gentle hand touch his face like that night in the restaurant after seeing Kat. Now, it was the touch of the breeze fluttering across his skin before it headed out toward the waters, standing still he felt a sense of release…

Then, his thoughts went back to the touching lady sitting on the bench behind him.

* * *

Kat took a breath, thinking of her sweet friend. Her fingers trembled as she eased the metal lid of the old lunchbox open. Its metal had rusted together making it a little tough but then it cracked open and she lifted it up to view inside. And there lay one half of a friendship necklace—the one she and Olivia had shared and this was Olivia's half. Her's was at home in her jewelry box, still a great memory she and her friend had shared.

The two of them had been best of friends because of their age. And as her sisters grew older, they all became friends. But first, at ten years old, it was she and Olivia and their cheap little shared necklaces.

By the time they'd come here on that last trip they no longer wore the little piece of jewelry. But, obviously, Olivia had never forgotten where their friendship started. Together, the two of them against the world.

Kat smiled and teared up at the same time. She was the big sister who loved her little sisters and always made sure they found their way if possible. Olivia had watched her stand up for them, help them through hard times of little girls and she'd seen her cry for them when they were hurt. Olivia had known when they dealt with her death that Kat would stand firm for them.

She held the necklace in her palm, her heart hurting. Her sisters were adults who'd done as Olivia hoped and found love along the way. She knew that her friend was smiling down from heaven right now.

She picked up the letter.

It had been gently folded, and on top it said, 'Always and Forever Best Friends.' Kat's heart squeezed again. "Yes, we are," she whispered as she carefully opened the envelope and read the handwritten note:

Kat,

We sat here yesterday... well, if you're reading this I have a feeling it's been more than a day. But for me, it was yesterday that we were sitting here on your bench looking out over the hillside leading down to the water you love. It's always been me and you against the world and I felt a strong feeling in my heart to write this. Never do we know what tomorrow holds, and for some reason

I feel that if you're reading this that my time on earth is done. Not sure why I feel it so strong like this but I do, and I feel a need to remind you of our talk yesterday.

Life holds a lot of surprises and a lot of dreams. God gave us yesterday to make memories for today, but remember because of our shared love of the Lord we will see each other again. But this is to remind you, my friend, who I think will be a wonderful workaholic building your dream restaurants for everyone to enjoy.

But I feel a need to remind you not to forget the important part of yesterday. We sat here and imagined our kids playing together on this mountainside, running and rolling and having a great time. You and me, playing with them while our husbands, whom we don't yet know, will be watching with us.

This is just my reminder to you not to forget that dream. Those children you'll love. You always dream of living on this ranch, raising your kids here. Your heart is also in cooking—and one day, you're going to have an amazing number of restaurants with your delicious dishes. But don't forget your kids on the hillside.

Your face glowed while talking about *your* future children. Your eyes twinkled talking about finding the right man where you could raise your children here on this Kona ranch that you love so much. As I lay in bed last night, your words kept ringing through me and I had to leave this note, wish you well, and say I hope you won't close your dreams off to children, to a husband, even owning a restaurant, even owning a hundred restaurants if you want. Dream big, be happy, and always know I cherished our time here on your hillside.

You will be in my heart, love you always,
Olivia

Kat's tears dropped onto the paper.

"Are you okay?"

She looked up, wiped her eyes as she met those of the concerned cowboy. He hadn't come her way, but he was looking at her with worry.

"This is a note about the last day we sat here and talked," Kat said, her voice trembled so she took a breath, then with determination halted its shakiness. "This is from the sweet Olivia, the strongest woman I've ever known. I just didn't realize it that day. Sitting here we talked about my goals in my life. I knew I would have at least two restaurants, was determined to, but I also dreamed of having a herd of kids."

"You did?"

"You sound shocked."

"Didn't mean to." He sat down beside her.

"Kids that I would raise here on this ranch. I love Kona and this ranch and that was my plan. The next day when I went to work cattle with the crew she rode one of the four-wheelers here and buried this note. She said she lay awake that night before and felt the need to leave it for me."

"This would be a great place to take a day trip to with your kids. They could romp and play with this amazing view before them. Why does her telling you that seem to make you so upset?"

"I'm not—okay, those were my plans before she found out she was ill and then died. My plans for my life changed on that journey with her, finding out she had a terminal cancer that would change her goals and mine."

The compassionate eyes of the cowboy locked with

hers. He took her hand in his, a warmth filled her.

"I'm so sorry for your loss. She sounds like an amazing person."

"She was."

"I understand where you are. When I lost Natalie, my plans changed instantly. There was no turning back to the things I'd wanted when she was alive."

"You get why I don't want to take that chance... I'm so sorry you lost her. That you'll never get those children you both wanted."

"I don't know that I can tell you completely that you shouldn't step out and find love. I've had it and there is nothing as beautiful to experience."

His words and the look in his eyes thinking of what he had and lost struck another strong strike to her heart. "Despite this sweet last wish from Olivia, there will never be any of my children playing on this hill or anywhere."

He turned toward her. "In that sweet letter she left you, she's telling you not to forget that, isn't she?"

She nodded. "Exactly." She folded the letter up gently, put it back in the box, closed the lid, letting her hands rest there as she looked down the hillside. In her mind she saw all those kids she'd once thought about playing there and her heart ached. "I thought I was going to have four or five kids."

"You did? Great number."

"Yes, I needed a slew of them to fill up this hillside. To work cattle and help run my restaurants that I dreamed about even back then. But the restaurants happened and the other won't." She met his gaze again.

"I bet your wife is looking down with Olivia wanting you to be happy."

"You're right. That's what Natalie would be wanting. But like you, it's not happening."

Their eyes locked and the emotions they'd turned up on the trip swirled around them. Despite the draw she felt and was sure he felt they were both on the same page.

CHAPTER SEVEN

Clay knew exactly what Olivia had wanted for her friend. He had had it, lost it, but loved every moment that he had been blessed with Natalie's love.

A very short ten years together that had been filled with fun, adventure, arguments, and sweet makeups of their loving relationship.

It had been short but what a life. They'd both had to adapt to their different lives. His love of ranching, horses and cattle. Her love of fishing, water and adventure on the deep sea. They'd been a perfect match until he'd lost her in that same deep sea she loved.

When he'd lost her, it had been the hardest thing he ever wanted to live through. He couldn't even imagine, and never even thought about trying to imagine living life with someone else. So here he was ranching just like he loved.

And lonely.

Now, where was his brain going as he looked at the beautiful woman sitting on the bench looking sad but determined.

"I think that Olivia was probably one of the smartest people I know," he said. "From the way I'm looking at it from the outside standing over here, she was one strong lady. At the young age y'all were when you were here on this mountain she was thinking about you. My Natalie didn't do that. She had no idea she was going to die so early. To be honest, I'm not sure if I would have wanted her to leave me a note—" His words cut to his core. "Actually, a note would have been great. Could have helped fill the hole in my heart." He couldn't say anything else.

Memories faded slowly, but surely aggravatingly in truth. In his heart and mind, he wanted to remember every moment they'd had together. But in the real world, he only remembered specific moments. But her laughter, the twinkle in her eyes, and the joy she had when she looked at him *or* caught a fish. He smiled and was able to think about the joy Natalie got when catching a giant Marlin especially.

"What's that smile about? You were looking so sad even probably sadder than I am sitting here with my memories. I get what Olivia did, and it touches my soul. What about you? I know my brother hurt terribly after losing Olivia. He ran away, taking Olivia with him in his heart, traveling to all the places they'd talked about before she died."

He stuffed his hands on his hips, put weight on one foot, and touched a rock with his other boot on the rough ground. "I worked cattle, threw myself into my job. I knew I couldn't stay where I was, so when your dad called, I came here. And he pointed me to this beautiful mountain top that was waiting for me."

Kat crossed over the rough ground to stand beside him. "I have a feeling that your sweet, talented wife would want you to have adventures again. You haven't been back out on the water since that terrible day?"

He looked out at the water as Kat came to stand

beside him, her auburn hair brushed his sleeve. "No," he forced the word out, trying to focus. "I *haven't* been on the water. I'll never fish again."

"Never?" Kat spun toward him, stumbled and was heading to the ground when Clay wrapped an arm around her and protectively pulled her against him, saving her precious container from Olivia, enclosed between them.

"Are you okay?" She nodded looking up at him. A stunning longing rolled through Clay, his arms tightened and he never wanted to let go.

"Clay," she whispered. "You have to go out on the water."

Shots of awareness flew through him like bullets of remembrance to an aching heart, a heart that never wanted to risk losing again. He loosened his grip on the beauty in his arms. "I won't. I can't."

She looked stunned as she looked up at him.

He was thankful he'd kept her from falling and losing her valuable box, but now he needed to get away yet their gazes were locked. Getting his brain back he gently released her and stepped back, desperately needing space or he might kiss her. "You remind me of her. The way you love fishing. Though, you look nothing like her. Both beautiful—in your own ways. But your love of the water is very similar." He felt more stable not having her in his arms. At least he could talk and needed his brain in another direction. "Did you ever think about being a professional fisherwoman?"

Kat grinned as she shook her head. "No way. I have no desire to be on the water like that all the time, trying to become the best of the best. I just enjoy it when I need it. I enjoy my cooking the most. But being on the water in my boat is where I find peace. Out there," she waved her hand to the water, "it's quiet and calm. The birds fly over. The small whales that resemble dolphins sometimes surround me on my early morning rides, as if they know me. They probably have no clue but for me it's a peace that fills me."

He was stunned by her soft words and the look in her eyes. The feel of her in his arms—he pushed that thought away. It was all confusing at the moment.

His heart pounding he forced his words out. "It actually sounds like a great place."

She cocked her head to the side. "It is, come out with me. On the water—it's where you need to be." Her eyes dug into him.

"Clay, I know I have Olivia watching me from heaven and from everything I know, you've got a beautiful lady watching you. And right now, I feel as if I have either her hand or Olivia's hand on my shoulder squeezing hard, telling me to urge you to come out on the water. It's where you need to be."

At her words his gut tightened then she placed her hand gently on his crossed arm and continued, "I've watched my sisters and my brother and parents go through the pain of losing Olivia and this is what I do. Believe me, sometimes you have to do something that helps you let go so you can move forward. Have you thought about that? Not letting go of your love, but letting go of what's holding you back from experiencing the joy of life. Me, I don't need a man to do that. I love cooking. Cooking is my sanctuary. That and the ocean."

"I have horses—"

"You say horses, but I think that you haven't let go." She looked up at the sky.

Her words were cutting deep, as her beautiful curling, rusty hair streamed down her back as she looked up at the sky. He needed to leave, to step away.

She let out a long breath of exasperation, it sounded like he felt. He gave up and looked up at the sky instead of her.

"They're watching," she said. "I can feel it."

He looked at her. "Do you ever feel down, sad? Let your loss get to you?"

"Yes, but no one sees it. I'm not one to back down, I meet problems straight on, and that's what I do in the mornings all alone just me and my world."

"Your world?"

She looked hard at him. "Cowboy, you *need* to get on the water. You need to believe me. I feel it with everything in me. You came with me today and helped when I needed it most. I have to pay you back and you have to believe me. You're going to come to the boat dock in the morning before five and I'll be there waiting for you."

His heart hammered and he realized that she might be right. It was time to get out on the water. "Five, I'll be there."

She smiled. "I'm sure you know how to dress for a day of fishing," she said. "Obviously, you had a wonderful wife who knew how to dress. I'm sure you probably still have shoes made for a boat. And probably a fishing shirt and a fishing hat versus your Stetson."

"Yes, I do," he said, and suddenly, he knew she was right. He needed, wanted to go out on the water with this woman. This woman who was touching him with truth. That's why his heart had started pounding. "You're right, it's time for me to get back in the saddle, the water. I'll be there for sure."

"Great. Alright. Let's load up. Get back down this mountain, this volcano beneath our feet."

"Let's do that."

They crossed to the horses and she placed her tools and her saddlebags back in place on Ladybug's back as he settled into the saddle of his horse. Then she looked up at him and in one very agile and capable move of a boot in a stirrup, a leg over and she settled into her saddle like the pro she was.

He was staring at her when her eyes locked with his. "Come on, cowboy, let's ride."

And they did just that. They rode. And for the first time in a long time, he was looking forward to morning… he would be sharing a sunrise with someone again. His heart ached, confused but all he knew was in the morning he wouldn't be alone.

CHAPTER EIGHT

Kat woke early the next morning and in the darkness was now on the boat waiting for the handsome cowboy to arrive. She'd realized yesterday that she was undeniably attracted to the strong man whether she wanted to be or not. It was an odd feeling for someone who wasn't planning on allowing romance or more to take over her life. But Clay was an amazing man and had obviously loved his fisherman of a wife desperately. Her heart ached for him, and it had been an instant revelation to her that she could help him.

She could *help* him. No romance involved.

She wasn't just thinking about how attractive he was and how much she had enjoyed the feel of his arms around her when she had lost her balance. Yes, she knew she was lying to herself when she tried to deny the attraction because the man drew her, like, nothing other than cooking had ever drawn her.

She breathed in the soft breeze rolling in over the dark waters that were, like she was, waiting for the first light of the new day. She focused on the walkway of the pier and then she saw him, the tall, lean, muscular man coming her way. He had no cowboy hat on but even in the dim light she recognized his walk, his build, and knew it was the man she was waiting on. Within seconds he was standing before her and the light of the boat showed that he wore a fishing shirt with a giant kingfish spread across his chest.

It was white, and the kingfish dazzled even in the dim light. He also had on fishing slacks, not denim jeans and he'd traded in his western boots for fishing shoes. He'd walked, stormed her way down the pier exactly like she thought he would look, surefooted and comfortable on the pier. The man knew what he was doing.

After all he had been married to a professional. She

smiled. "Good morning," she said as he reached the boat.

"Good morning," he said, looking down at her. "I'm here, and it looks like you are too."

Her smile spread wider. "Come aboard, cowboy. I mean, fisherman."

With that, he stepped onto the back part of the boat, didn't even have to grab anything for balance, which meant he knew exactly how to hold his balance on a boat. He took the step down onto the small step then, looking like a professional getting on a boat, he was standing before her on equal ground.

"That was smooth," she said.

"I've done it a few times."

"I can tell." She smiled. "Alright, I've got the boat ready and a great lunch packed with drinks, and I've got amazing rods and reels as you can see." She waved her hand upward to the poles sticking out from the rack connected to the canvas and steel roof.

He followed her wave, looking up above the seat, where the canvas covering was, and all the fishing poles stuck in the holes that held them up to salute the sky where they would ride on the trip until needed for fishing.

"Those are some amazing reels you've got on those rods."

"I was just testing you to see if you knew what you were looking at."

He laughed. "Yes. Believe me. I know what I'm looking at. I handled many great reels in my earlier days."

"That's awesome. I can't wait to watch you in action."

He shook his head. "No. I want to watch you in action. I also know when you're on a boat fishing for certain fish, the boat needs a driver. And, yes, I'm good with horses, but I'm good with a boat too."

She smiled. Couldn't help it. "I thought you were." The man was probably good at whatever he took on. Her gaze went to his smiling lips—then she turned and grabbed the steering wheel. "I'll let you set us free from the dock. I see the glow rising on the horizon so it's time to let loose."

He said nothing so she looked over her shoulder to

see him unwrap the rope, drop it inside the boat, step to the other side and did the same. This boat was docked by the back not the sides so no walking to the front to undo a rope. He turned and found her watching.

"Ready when you are." Then walked to stand next to the bench seat where she was at.

"Perfect." She pulled the lever, and off they went slowly forward then turned at the corner and headed toward the exit. The sun was up now, and she saw the shock on the faces of the fishermen as they passed by and she waved at them like she always did. The difference this morning was that they had never seen anybody on this boat with her before. Especially a long, tall fisherman.

She almost said cowboy but today he was a fisherman. She liked it. She grinned at him and caught him looking at the men on the docks with their hands on their hips openly watching them. "We're starting rumors. You know? All these fishermen that I wave at each morning have never seen anyone ride in this boat with me."

"Seriously?"

She nodded. "This is my boat. My peaceful place and that's why you're with me today. We're going to have a great peaceful day on the water." She almost teared up knowing this was where she needed to be and hoped it was right for him.

He was standing there beside her watching her and might have seen the glisten of the tears in her eyes. He put a hand on the seat back shifted so he was now facing the horizon. "You're right. I'm going to think positive, and it's going to be a great day."

There was a sound in his voice that drew her to look at him as he looked toward the rocks at the entrance where they were heading. His wife had obviously enjoyed the adventure of the calling water. She wondered if she'd felt the peace of the water that Kat was heading for this morning.

Kat's heart rumbled when he turned his head and caught her looking. The cowboy was amazingly handsome but that wasn't what she saw in that moment, it was the unsettled man behind all that gloss.

"We're going to take it slow this morning. I'm going to show you what draws me here at this time of day. *This* is the start of a new day," she said softly as she waved a hand before them. "This is where I find peace like no other."

She looked at him as a calmness of the ocean came over her like it always did. She hoped he felt it. His eyes were on the rocks on the side of land running along the ocean's edge. At her pause he looked at her.

"Peace is what you need."

"Don't we all?" She drilled her gaze into him, since he'd tried to deny what she saw moving in his eyes. "Instead of going straight out there to that beautiful water we're turning right." They'd just reached the opening to the ocean. "This is where the other boaters let their engines roar then shoot out there into the bay where the huge fish roam."

She turned the steering wheel and they headed along the side of the beautiful lava rocks where the ocean waters rushed in then spewed water up and out toward the sky and the calming feeling filled her. She loved this spot.

"So we're going by the lava rocks, watch what happens," she said, looking at him.

He did as she asked and looked out at rocks as the boat cruised in the water, passing by them slowly. "You watch them and relax?" He looked at her. "You're really into trying to get me to relax. I'm okay on the water. I'm not holed up in my house mourning. Instead of being on my ranch, dealing with life, I'm here with you today on the water."

"You intrigue me, cowboy. You are determined to hide—"

"I'm not hiding anything, I'm on the water."

"Okay, it's actually none of my business, so I'll not go there. I'm going to enjoy my morning, and hope you enjoy it too." With that she focused on driving and watched the water roll in, slam into the rocks then spew up toward heaven. Instantly the beauty of it, the excitement of it, most importantly the calmness of it washed over her. She closed her eyes, and let the calmness soak over her.

She glanced at him as he was watching her then turned and watched the water. "When Olivia died I came here. I ran away and got in my boat and I let this be my place. You know sometimes we have hardships that slam into us like a hard wave that tries to sweep us away. That's what was happening to me, and I came here, like that water hitting the rocks, it's like my emotions hitting them then flying up into the air and turning beautiful. Just look at that."

A huge wave rolled in as she was talking. It hit the rocks and spewed but some of it went through the holes in the rock then burst upward through a hole like a volcano erupting and spewed white foaming water into the rising golden rays of the sun.

It looked like golden glitter spewing in the sky. "This is why I come here. That is Olivia telling me to let my sorrow go. Let it hit those rocks, like they hit me in my heart then let them go. It's as if she is grabbing them, then throwing them up into the air and God turns them into sparkles. And I breathe again."

They were staring at each other.

"So you, the strong one needed some release."

It wasn't a question but a statement. "Yes."

"You keep everything hidden?"

"I try."

"This isn't just where you let sorrow go."

"No. If I'm feeling really agitated because I'm not being able to fix someone's problem, yeah that's me, I'm a fixer. This is where I deal with things. Not out there in public."

"So those rocks take your anger and frustration and then spew them up and out."

She smiled. "Yes. Maybe it sounds silly—"

"No, I get it." The look on his face and in his eyes was such an unbelievable emotion.

She was suddenly afraid she'd made a mistake. But she hadn't. "Like Olivia does for me, your sweet wife wants to do the same. Let her take your anger and throw it up into the air and make glitter out of it." He blinked and stared out at the rocks. She watched his strong jaw clench, then a huge wave hit the rocks. In that instant the water then came out in a mass of sparkling drops spewing into the sunlight as he watched. And she saw his shoulders relax. She prayed that he had just felt what she hoped he'd felt.

Then he turned and looked at her. "I felt Natalie do just what you said. My fisherman wife grabbed everything while smiling and threw it in the air."

"It feels great doesn't it?"

He gave a tender smile. "Yep."

"Did she tell you to 'Let it go?'"

He nodded. "Yes, in the same growling voice she had when she was frustrated because she had to let a huge fish go back into the waters. To freedom."

Kat's heart squeezed. "I get that. I'm not happy when I've caught the best fish in the sea and I have to release it back. I have to give it freedom but I understand I can't have them all on my wall as trophies. I have to let them go and their destiny isn't mine to determine."

They stared at each other as the water rocked the boat and she glanced to make sure they weren't heading for a crash. Then she looked back at him. "Do you feel better?" Unable to stop herself she reached out grasped his upper arm and gave a gentle squeeze, felt the muscle tense then she put her hand back on the steering wheel where it belonged. And hoped her touch didn't cause tension to return.

"You, you get it."

She shrugged at his words. "I get it to a point. Olivia was my best friend. But, I can't imagine if it were the person I loved with all my heart. I don't want to ever do that. I'm so sorry that you did."

"We all know going into marriage that one of the two will lose a spouse at some time. Till death do we part."

"I know that, but not me because I'm not ever marrying. But yes, if married, one of the two is going to lose. And like Olivia said, on her deathbed as she placed her hand on my jaw. "Life has hurts but love and joys live on. Love makes even a small time worth it." Tears came into her eyes as she said the words, remembering. Kat swallowed hard, she was here to help this man.

Clay had stepped to the edge of the boat holding onto the rail with one hand. "You haven't told anyone that have you?"

"What?"

"That you can't let yourself find love because you don't want to feel more…"

"More?" She stared straight ahead, heart pounding. Was the man reading her mind?

"She was telling you to let go so you could one day know what she'd known for a short time."

She stared at him. "I didn't say that."

"Didn't need to. It's clear. She loved you dearly, like you loved her. But she knew you like no one else knows you. That you hold everything back, in order to be the strong one for everyone."

"What's wrong with that?" The man had taken her morning of helping him and turned it on her. She held his gentle eyes and said firmly, "I am strong."

His lips lifted. "Yes, you are. I am too, but I know that one day I'll move forward. Natalie would want me to. I simply wasn't in a rush. I lost Natalie and am on no one's timeline but my own. But I knew that one day I'd live again. Fully, if I wanted to."

"Wanted to?"

"Yes. I'm living now, but came here to be still."

Be still and know that I am God... the verse played through her mind and she swallowed more emotions. *Breathe...*

"Thank you for bringing me out here. I feel it." He smiled.

"Good. After almost five years I realize that there's not anyone I need to stand up for, to help be happy again. My brother's happy, my two sisters are happy, my dad and mom are happy. Then you showed up and I felt I needed to help you. I hope I did."

"Yes. You know, your dad is a smart man. He knew I needed to be here on Kona, on the ranch up there on the mountain. I don't know if he knew I needed to be out here on the water too, but—" He looked around. "As much as I want to say I shouldn't be here. Thank you. I get it now. And yes, I feel more peace. And I think we've made two ladies happy today."

A smile she couldn't stop burst across her face and her heart. "Yes, we have. And the sun has risen and it's a beautiful day. It's awesome." She paused getting a grip on her flare of emotions. "So now that they're smiling and we get it and I see some relief in your eyes. I feel like I've paid you back for taking me up there yesterday to find the letter from my sweet Olivia. To your relief I believe we're even. But, since you've helped me, now we're going to leave these pretty rocks and water behind and I'm taking us out to the middle."

"The middle?"

"Yes, you've got to see the whales." She looked out toward the open waters and felt great relief. "There is more than sorrow and relief here on Kona. There's deep open water, adventure, and joy. And still, it's not all about catching the big giant Marlin that people come from all over the world to try and catch. There's also peace and fun swarming in these beautiful blue waters my favorite whales in all the world are here. They look like dolphins with a bump on their foreheads. Pilot whales. And you are going to get to experience them. I have a feeling they're going to show up."

"Pilot whales? They sure put joy in your voice and your amazing eyes."

His words struck... amazing eyes. She looked at him, and couldn't breathe. Her heart thundered. "Yes," she managed to get out. She focused on where she was taking him, not on the man who struck her heart in ways she didn't—couldn't want. "So hang on, here we go."

Then she turned the boat toward the open water, shifted the gear, and they blasted forward toward the open waters. And with the breeze hitting them full force, Clay laughed.

And her heart clinched as she looked at him, hair waving in the wind and excitement in his eyes that connected with hers. "I have been wondering when you were going to press the gas. I knew this boat had speed."

The tall man hadn't moved, lost balance or fallen when out of her overwhelming internal revelation to herself she'd blasted from their simple drifting on the waters into full throttle.

No, the cowboy fisherman stood solid on the boat. He knew exactly how to stand as they roared across the water toward the center of the bay.

And she had to tell *herself* to breathe... and hold on.

CHAPTER NINE

He couldn't believe what he had just felt, and he knew he hadn't expected it. He'd come determined to be the man that Natalie loved. She'd love seeing him dressed like a fisherman. Loved having him on the water with her, and he had dressed for her today. Now he realized he'd liked Kat seeing that he knew how to dress for the water.

Kat was amazing. When he watched that water slam into all that lava rock spewing up into the air, he understood why she came here as the sun was rising. The way the sparkles of the drops in the air caught the sunlight had him actually feeling relief, and that made him feel Natalie nudging him, telling him to get up and move forward.

Suddenly it hit him that he had just made Natalie happy because he actually felt like he'd taken a step forward. He smiled and felt that he'd taken that step because of this beautiful woman standing in front of him. The woman who'd known exactly what he needed.

Now as they raced across the harbor, more fishing boats were joining them out on the bay. All were making their own waves in the water as they headed out to different places on the calm waters. He relaxed, then stepped behind the windshield to stand beside Kat. It eased the wind from slamming into him as he watched the water flying by.

Kat glanced at him, smiled, then also relaxed with her hip resting against the seat-bench, her hands still in control as together they watched the beautiful blue waters of Kona Bay fly in the wind.

And then suddenly she slowed the boat, and they were drifting. "See them?"

He saw what looked like a dolphin swimming in the water, then several of them suddenly came to the surface. "Yes, you're amazing. You knew where they'd be?"

"Yes, they're Pilot whales, they look like dolphins with humps on their heads. They're great entertainers."

She was right, they were swimming and diving all around them as if it was their job or joy to entertain. He laughed. "It's like they've been hired to entertain us."

Kat turned the engine off, and she joined him at the back to watch the show. He felt the beauty surround him with the whales and the lady standing beside him. "You know exactly what you're looking for. It's almost as if they were waiting on you."

Her expression warmed brightly as her eyes met his. "They're not waiting on me, but, I can sit here and they show up most of the time. Okay," she said and sighed. "I hope I don't drive you crazy with all the things I'm pointing out but when I'm hurting or angry all this helps me. It's as if I go there by the rocks, and I let my emotions spew out and my anger fly up into the air and it turns into sparkly jewels, glittering in the sky surrounding me. And then here with all these sweet, beautiful, dolphin-looking whales looking at me, it's like a gift to me."

"I get it," he said. "I really do. Thank you for

bringing me."

She looked serious again. "You're welcome. Now, you want a tour of the island from this view instead of up there on the mountain top?" She pointed up, and there, in the distance, was their hill. They were far enough away that he couldn't see the bench, but he knew that was their hill. "Yes. I do."

She stood up. "Alright. Then here we go."

* * *

They'd enjoyed a few more hours on the water talking, sometimes just the quietness of it and the peace settled in around them. They saw one of the boats catch a huge Blue Marlin and paused to sit there at a distance enjoying the show. The fight that went on between the fishermen and the huge fish was amazing.

"So, you enjoy doing that just like Natalie did," he said. He'd stopped watching the fight and was watching her expression as she watched the fight between fishermen and huge fish.

She turned sparkling eyes on him. "I do. I love a

challenge. I can't help it. I've caught several over the years but I thoroughly enjoy the challenge whether I catch it or not."

"It's the challenge that pulls you in?"

"Yes, but I catch other things also. I'm not just after Blue Marlin. You don't fish at all?"

He shrugged. "I was really only there for my wife. She loved it, like you. But if she was on the water, she wanted to fish. If you want to catch something, I can drive the boat."

She waved her hand as if waving off the idea. "No, but thanks though."

He felt a challenge well up inside of him. "Are you sure? I am a great driver."

She cocked her head and shot a look back at him. "Are you sure about that?"

"Believe me, I can make any kind of move in this boat you'll need me to make when you snag a giant Blue Marlin or any other fish out there that decides to snag whatever you want to toss out there for it."

"So, is that a challenge?"

He smiled. "Actually, yes. You said I was the first

person to be on this boat with you. That means you've never fished for a Marlin from it. Why not now? Come on, toss something out."

She stood up and looked at the poles above them, then grinned at him. "Okay, let's do this." She reached up, standing on the bottom rung of the seat to be tall enough to reach the pole but had it down instantly.

"You want the other two?" he asked as she placed that one in the side slot on the right side of the backend of the boat.

"You know I do." Yes, he did know. Natalie always started with at least four poles, with the lines at different lengths, the lures slightly different, all going after the fish that she hoped would be swimming below the surface.

He reached up and took two poles down as she strode to the spot where she placed the first one. She set the line up with a lure she pulled from a bucket in the corner of the boat. He walked to the other side and set each pole in a hole, waiting and ready.

He watched her, memories coming back of all the times he'd watched Natalie prepare everything for the day. There on her face was the expression of excitement for the challenge. He stood back, memories hammering down on him that he hadn't been prepared for. Memories he was prepared to tear him up inside and didn't want her to see. She got the lure attached then let the line out. He'd stepped to the steering wheel and was now, like he was supposed to be doing, moving the boat slowly through the water as she prepared the poles he'd set up for her.

"So what are you fishing for?" he asked, forcing his words out casually.

"Well, I could fish for anything, but we're out here, first time I have my own driver, and they just caught that big Marlin, so we're going for a big boy." She hitched a brow and cracked a huge teasing smile at him.

And he laughed. *Laughed*. Relief flowed through him. "I thought you were going to go after something more adventurous. But I know how to drive in order for you to have a chance of catching your Marlin. And today is a great peaceful day for trolling across the ocean, watching for the birds. The birds that tell us where the small bait fish are that attract the Marlin. I'm prepared for trolling and enjoying a hard day of fishing." He winked.

She laughed this time. "You do know how it goes. It's almost exactly like we were just doing but the difference is the moment I hear that line start spinning— excitement snags me and takes over. Believe me, I'll be in that seat strapped in and ready within seconds."

He laughed. "I'm sure you will be. And I know my job then too, I'll have the other ones tied up and out of the way then go back to driving while you, Kat, hopefully catch your all-time biggest catch ever."

Grinning, they stared at each other and suddenly it slammed into him that he was smiling. And ready to have some fun...

Her expression sobered. "Are you okay?"

He nodded and grinned again. "I'm great. Really great. Let's get to trolling."

She smiled. "Let's do this. I'll be standing here watching, waiting for that reel to start screaming, signaling a Marlin has taken my bait. Honestly, the way I look at it is that it's my lucky day, no matter if I catch anything or not. I mean, yesterday and this morning have been great."

He pulled his gaze off of her and looked out ahead, then at the screen of the fish finder, watching the depth line they'd be traveling and knowing that yes, this was a really great day.

* * *

After they been trolling for an hour, Kat moved past Clay to the front of the boat and looked at him through the clear windshield. What a day this had turned into. "I'm grabbing a snack before I catch my mammoth Marlin. Would you like something?"

She leaned down and lifted two plastic bags. One had sandwiches in it. One had fruit. "I'm having a peanut butter sandwich but there's turkey too."

"Peanut butter is good for me."

She laughed. "Okay. A man after my own heart."

He took the sandwich and the bottle of water she handed him as she sat on the bench beside him. She took one bite and he still had his hand on the steering wheel and was taking a bite when she heard it—heard the reel start screaming—as it was called, signaling that a

Marlin had taken the bait. She dropped her sandwich, shot to her feet, loving the sound.

In an instant she'd raced to the rod that was bending over with the strain and weight of the Marlin on the other end. She grabbed the rod with both hands, feeling the strain as the reel continued to sing. She instantly went to work getting it under control, leaning forward with the flow then pulling back and feeling the tension then giving it room again. Getting a huge fish in was an art, a skill that was learned and loved by her.

Both hands working, she backed up carefully toward her place in the waiting seat. Excitement filled her then she realized she hadn't thought about the other rods and their lines that could now get in the way of her line that had the Marlin on it. One glance over and she saw Clay had one reeled in and the other he was taking care of. The lines had to be out of her way and that was part of his job.

"Thank you," she said, thrilled that the cowboy knew his business.

Nothing but her and the large fish and open water with the line stretching from her to the Marlin.

"Here you go," Clay said, gently placing the belt that would give her relief, it went between her waist and the rod as she held it away from her body while Clay moved the belt around her and buckled it in place. Feeling his hands on her—on the fishing belt took her focus off the fish as their gazes locked together. She couldn't move, suddenly wishing she didn't have a fish on the line holding her back from the kiss she wanted—

"Work it, Kat. Get it under control, you've got this," he said, helping to get the end of the rod into the holder that was now attached to her hips. "I've got the wheel."

That said he headed to the dashboard and she— well, short of breath and a storming heart taking over— looked out at the ocean as the Blue Marlin burst from the water and reached for the sky.

The size and strength of the beauty took her whole concentration, thank goodness.

"That's a huge fish," Clay said, expressing what she was thinking and feeling.

"Yes, and beautiful." Her muscles worked hard, very hard, working the reel, and then the fighter blasted from the water again. Kat leaned back pulling, fighting as the blue beauty spun in the air and Kat smiled the instant she felt the line come break and knew the Marlin had won. Breathing hard she stood still, her smile wide as the amazing creature dove like a champion back into the blue waters where it belonged and quickly the waters calmed as it swam away.

Then, there was a hand on her shoulder and a light squeeze that sent electricity shooting through her that hooking the Marlin hadn't caused. "That was spectacular. Both the fish and you."

Kat didn't look at him, had to get hold of her reaction to his touch. "And that's why I enjoy it." She closed her eyes, then looked at him and he smiled. And her ragging heart—calmed. "Now, it's time to go home."

"Yes, it is." He gave one more gentle squeeze to her shoulder and drew his hand back. "Have you ever thought about taking that competitive talent into professional competition? You have the skills."

She relaxed. "I snagged him, didn't catch him, but no, I only do it for a fun challenge."

He gave a nod. "I think that's good. There's a difference when you're fishing for the fun of it. Competition isn't for everybody, but Natalie loved it."

"That's great. But I'm only in competition with myself, less tension and as you see, out here I'm all in for no tension."

"I get it. Look, I can't go often because I do have that ranch of your dad's to take care of but anytime you need a driver, you just let me know."

She laughed and before she realized what she was doing she reached out and hugged him. "Thank you so much for coming today and for being my driver." She released him and stepped away—heart thundering once again by her reactions to the cowboy fisherman who now looked a bit shook up. Just like she felt.

* * *

Clay froze, just stood there shocked as Kat dropped her arms and stepped back then spun and went to work cleaning up. She might not have thought anything of the hug, but he hadn't felt arms around him in a long time.

And it wasn't just any arms around him. It was this beautiful woman whom he admired and had connected with.

Get your head on straight. He took a slow breath and then looked at her as she rolled up the reel, preparing it to be put away.

"Ready to head in?" he forced out.

She looked at him. 'The day can't get any better, so let's go."

"I agree. That'll get me back to the ranch in time to make sure everything's going smooth."

"Yes. And I can go to the restaurant tonight to work."

"Right." With that, he went back to the steering wheel, then looked over his shoulder, and she was holding onto the metal railing, gave him a thumbs up so he shifted gears and they sped toward land. And steady ground.

CHAPTER TEN

Kat went to work that night after spending the day on the boat with Clay. She'd enjoyed herself and knew he had too. Even though it was a busy night and lots of work, her thoughts repeatedly went back to the cowboy.

The cowboy who'd helped her fish for a Marlin. The thought had her smiling throughout the evening every time she thought about it.

She caught her waiting staff watching her and talking and was pretty sure they were wondering what had happened to keep her smiling. They were great since they let her enjoy herself without asking and she was glad about that. She wasn't exactly sure what she would say if someone asked her why she felt so uplifted.

She wasn't sure how to handle the thought that wouldn't leave her mind... her mind that was wondering what life might be like if she had Clay around all the time?

And realizing that it was a thought worth thinking about. Even though she knew it could put her at risk of losing more than she wanted to ever lose.

Yet, the warmth surrounding her wouldn't go away. That warmth was the feel of his arms around her, standing there on the boat together.

* * *

Clay could not get her off his mind. He worked hard the next few days, riding, roping, branding with all of his cowboys who knew he was a hard worker, but he knew that they were all wondering why he was working them extra hard.

And he didn't say anything. They needed to know that working hard was a gift and needed. And if you worked on this ranch, a must-have.

So yes, he worked them hard and himself, trying to keep his brain from going back to being on the water with Kat and sitting on that hillside also.

By Saturday afternoon he'd had enough and after a shower he shaved then dressed. He'd pulled out some starched shirt and jeans, a pair of nice boots, topped it off with a straw Stetson then stared at himself in the mirror.

"You look like the cowboy you are and not a fisherman." He was a cowboy straight up. He was a fisherman only when he was on the water with the woman who wanted him to be there… He'd gotten no call inviting him back out and that was fine. Still unable to stop himself because the truth was he didn't want to stop himself, he climbed into his truck and headed toward Kona.

Headed to the Café By The Seaside. Headed toward Kat.

He knew he might be getting himself in trouble, but… he wasn't going to deny the truth. There was something there between him and Kat whether he'd been looking for it or not.

And it could just be that they both had suffered loss and found a connection through that. But he was not one to ever just sidestep anything. He got things done. And that meant he needed to see Kat again. Needed to just see if she looked like he felt. One look and he'd know if she'd felt something momentarily or if, like him, was still not over that hug and those two remarkable days they'd shared.

He thought about it all the way down the winding roads to town. And then he parked. As if meant to be there was an available parking space at the Café By The Seaside's parking lot. It was meant to be.

He climbed out of his truck and strode to the entrance, where the same smiling hostess smiled bigger when she spotted him.

"Hello," she said, excitement rang out in her voice and eyes. "You're back."

He laughed. "Yes, Lettie, you were right, the food is really great here, so isn't it normal to have repeat diners?"

She picked up a menu. "You remembered my name."

"I'm great with names, especially if someone makes an impression and you did. You said you had a great chef and you gave me the perfect table by the water. It was great the other night. You were right on both. Does that table happen to be available tonight so I can order another great meal from that chef?"

Lettie laughed. "You're *good*. And yes, on both counts. Yes, all the food is great. We *do* have the most excellent chef in all the world and tonight is your lucky night, she's here and the table near the kitchen door and the water is open. Follow me, please." She winked, then spun and he followed.

They walked through the open area, past the singers and to the far corner where she'd hit his request on target he could see the entrance to the kitchen and that had been his goal.

She glanced around. "It still has a great view here. I'll let your waiter come take your order, but we're glad to have you back." She leaned forward. "And in all honesty, I can't lie, someone saw you out on the water with our boss, Kat. She's said nothing about it but has been all smiles this week. Now, I'll go back to my hostess spot. Have a great evening."

"You too," he said as she walked away smiling. So, Kat had been all smiles. The thought settled on him, as he looked out from over the lava rock and swirling water as it washed and swirled around down below his table. The moon was high in the sky and glimmered on the water all the way to the edge of the world. His thoughts stayed on Kat, not sure how she would feel about Lettie's remarks, but it was clear her employees obviously cared about her.

He looked around. There were a few less customers but it was later than it had been last time he was here. Closing time was in an hour so he better get an order in soon. His waiter, not the same one he'd had before, but another nice young lady, came, and he asked her what the chef's special was that evening, when she handed him the menu.

She said, "Oh, she's working on some things, but the last great thing she did is now on the menu." And she pointed to exactly what he'd had last time.

He smiled. "I had that and it was amazing. I think tonight I want to try some of her other things. Maybe seafood."

"Oh, she has seafood and steak, like that one. But she has amazing fish tacos."

"Then, I'll have the fish tacos. And water."

The waitress grinned, spun and headed in through the door to place his order.

He tried not to stare at the door, instead looked back out to the peaceful water. The reflections from the torches mounted on the outside of the deck played across the water as a gentle breeze came in with the soft waves.

Peaceful. The tension that he had been feeling all week eased as he sat there. It was clear that the woman had an eye for easing people's stress. Their pain. It was clear to him now that she had purposefully picked this spot for her restaurant.

Still, he had a feeling that even if she'd not been able to purchase this spot on the water with the comforting water washing in over the rocks, she would have created a luring atmosphere on her own... this peaceful song of gentle melody, that eased everyone's stress.

"Good evening."

The familiar voice zipped through him. His insides jumped, his blood pressure skyrocketed, and his pulse almost burst from beneath his skin as he turned his gaze to the beautiful woman smiling down at him. "Hello," he managed.

"So, you've decided to come have something to eat again."

He nodded. "I did. You probably don't have time but would you like to sit down?"

She glanced toward the kitchen then back at him. "It's almost closing time and you ordered tacos tonight, our specialty. So, my amazing chef can handle it from here." She waved at the waitress who came over smiling. "Tell Chef Ridge to do the order, and actually double it. I'm going to sit here for dinner tonight."

"Wow, you're going to sit down and eat here?" the waitress asked excitedly.

"Yes, I am. It is my restaurant, you know." She laughed, making Clay grin watching her, and the waitress was obviously excited.

The waitress hurried away to get water, he assumed and tell the chef the news.

"Do you not eat at your own restaurant often?"

She grinned. "Not with a cowboy. In case you haven't figured it out we just started a bunch of rumors."

He laughed. "I kind of got that. Lettie was also very welcoming when she seated me."

"Is that okay? Rumors start from almost nothing."

Almost nothing wasn't what he was feeling. He'd come down the mountain to see if he experienced the emotions, the crazy waves of connection that had hung with him since they'd gone out on the boat. The overwhelming connection he felt toward this beautiful lady.

"You have a way about you, Kat," he said, and meant it. "A way of choosing the perfect place for your restaurants, the perfect people to work for you—represent you, and where you fish."

Her expression softened beautifully. "Thank you. I love it all." She leaned forward on the table and cupped her hands together.

"I can tell." His hands were not on the table, thank goodness, or he would have wanted to gently place his hands on hers.

It was a feeling he hadn't felt since losing Natalie and never before or since. That fact alone had him stunned. Was it because of the boat, and memories colliding together of Natalie and Kat—two women who loved the excitement on the water?

"Have you been thinking about our fishing trip?" she asked.

"Actually, I can't get it off my mind."

Her serious gaze locked onto him. "Me too. I mean, thank you. I needed that as much as you did. Do you realize that when I came home from my sisters' weddings, both times should have been happy moments in time? But it was almost as sad to me as losing Olivia. However, this morning, when I went out on my boat at sunrise no unhappy emotions went with me. No anger or frustration was there for me to release it was just a peaceful time. I watched the waters wash in, slam against the rocks and the water was beautiful spraying up to the heavens. And I was smiling the whole time."

Clay didn't even try to stop as he placed his hand over hers and squeezed gently. "I'm so glad because you helped me on that trip so that's one reason I had to come and see you. To see if you'd experienced anything like I experienced."

She looked at his hand gently cupping hers. "I did. This morning out there on my ocean in my boat alone, I felt peace." Tears welled in her eyes. "And I loved it."

He was speechless then offered, "Anytime you want a partner out there just let me know."

Her lips lifted into a gentle smile. "I liked being out on the water with you."

"Right back at you."

"Here's your waters," the waitress said as she set the glasses on the table after they'd let go of each other's hands. "Your fish tacos should be done shortly."

They smiled as she headed to the kitchen.

"Sorry about the hand-holding. I didn't mean to cause a problem."

"It's okay, relax."

He was trying but he knew now he could lose his heart to this lady. Something he knew she wasn't or at least hadn't admitted she could do the same. And would he risk giving in to the feeling he knew she stirred in him now.

"I'm glad you came," she said.

Those simple words settled around him. "I'm glad you feel that way. I'm glad I came too."

Their food was delivered, placed quietly before them, and then with a smile, they were left alone once more.

Kat took a breath. "I have to say what's going on between us is complicated for me and for you, I'm sure."

"Yes. For both of us, like you said."

She tilted her head slightly looking at him. "Right now, let's eat and then maybe we can talk later or not at all, whatever you want to do."

"Great idea," he agreed and they both picked up a taco and bit in.

His mind wasn't on the food but on what came next. Was his heart really where he believed it to be…?

CHAPTER ELEVEN

The sound of gentle waves rolling in, soft music playing and her restaurant was packed, but best of all,she was sitting on the edge of it all enjoying an amazing fish taco with a man.

Not just any man but Clay. And loving every moment.

She looked at the handsome cowboy. "You know, not often do I sit down in my restaurants. I'm usually working. Thank you for giving me the opportunity to enjoy this." She looked out across the waters coming onto the rocks that the flames from the torches lit along the railing and the sparkling moonlight lit the waves beautifully.

"So why don't you ever sit down in your restaurants? I mean, you created them."

His interest made her happy. "I love cooking, I'm a bit obsessed with it. But, since losing Olivia and not being on a ranch at all, well, cooking is my big distraction."

"So sitting down and enjoying an evening at them isn't on the list. Surely this isn't the first time."

His question hit home. When was the last time she herself had enjoyed her own restaurant like a customer was known to do? Emotion filled her. "Once a year my sisters and I meet at my beautiful restaurant there in Star Gazer Island and celebrate our love of Olivia. We have the table down the side of the river that winds down with tables at certain levels. We always sit at the one that's lowest. There you have the perfect view of the ocean as the river flows into it, free to spread out and not be contained by boundaries. The view is outstanding. The sunsets are like no others. And it was Olivia's favorite spot."

"It sounds fantastic. Why don't you do it more?"

She toyed with her napkin. "We meet there once a year because it was Olivia's favorite place and we toast our sweet friend then talk about our year and our goals. That was Olivia's last wish for us as a group, talking about our year and what is to come. Staying connected. We added the toast to her to start it with because she was so important to us. Then we talk and remember the important request she made and what the impact of doing what she asked of us was. And you helped me do one of the most important requests from Olivia when you helped me dig up that treasure. And that's the only other time I've sat down at a table in my restaurant in a very long time."

Their gazes locked and she realized for the first time in forever that she'd told someone other than her sisters the deepest things in her heart. She never opened up to anyone but this man. This cowboy was easy to talk to. There was care in his eyes, understanding. "Do you have things like that?"

* * *

Clay had enjoyed the evening more than he'd believed he ever could. Now he thought about her question. "You saw it the other day before you took me out on our wonderful boat ride—the ride that changed my life when you helped me let go of some of the emotions that held me back. You're seeing it now, me sitting here. I didn't go out to restaurants anymore. Your dad got me here the first time and I'm thankful for that. But this time I'm sitting here in your restaurant because I wanted to be here. And I'm enjoying it very much."

The gentle smile that lit up her face touched him deeply. "I'm glad to be of help."

Needing a distraction from that smile he took a bite of his taco.

"Oops," she said as she reached over and wiped a small dot of sauce off the edge of his lip.

Her touch was like a warm ray of sunshine that instantly ignited his pulse. He smiled. "Sorry, but thanks for taking care of me."

She hitched a brow. "You know, that simple little thing I just did is going to start more rumors churning."

He laughed, loving her humor and the teasing smile. They had fun together. What was happening between them wasn't just about the deep-hearted moments they'd shared. "I've seen a few of those romance movies that always have the moment one reaches out and wipes away a drop of something on the other one's face after they're eating or drinking hot chocolate. So you're saying maybe your employees might be getting ideas." His thoughts went to the smiling waitress who'd been smiling earlier as she'd walked away.

Kat nodded. "We're both in the same boat. Not planning on enjoying our time spent with each other quite so much."

"True," he replied, knowing she was right.

"But, I don't care," she added, surprising him. "It's been really fun and I needed it. Needed your help... with everything."

His heart paused then kicked him in the ribs because there was no way to deny what he felt. "Yes," he forced out. "That's actually what brought me here tonight to find out if what we—well, me—what I'm feeling is real or not. I wasn't sure until now, seeing you again. You can say back off if you want to. But I won't lie, because I know now that I am very drawn to you in a deep way."

Her expression grew serious. "Are you sure?"

"I've never felt what I feel around you about anyone other than what I felt around Natalie. I never expected to feel drawn to someone like that ever again." It was so very true. "I'm not putting pressure on you. I'm just letting you know straightforwardly what I'm feeling. I don't date, haven't even thought about it until now."

"Then we're literally in the same boat. I have gone out a few times, but I am committed to growing my business, but, Clay, I'm committed to never knowing the loss that my brother felt or that you felt. I'm never going to chance losing someone I gave my heart to. I don't want to feel what you've felt."

He nodded, and it touched his heart but in a way he hadn't thought it would. She would never know what real love felt like. His love for Natalie had lived on and he was so much more alive and blessed than if he'd not risked loving her. But that was him, this was Kat's call. "I get it. That's why I wasn't sure about whether I should come tonight and tell you what was going on in my brain, my heart."

She remained silent but studied him with her green

eyes, beautiful and drawing him in without even trying. He knew now he wanted her to know love. He'd been so blessed to have had Natalie's love and been able to love her back with all of his heart.

"So the truth is," Kat said at last. "As crazy as it sounds after telling you all that, I actually like the feeling being around you gives me. I can't promise anything more though."

His heart was pounding an uplifted rhythm. She was being honest. He had been honest with her and she was returning that to him. They were on equal ground. What if she fell in love with him?

What if he fell in love and she walked away?

The questions raced through him. But the look in her eyes, the caring, the truthfulness flowed from her, and he loved it. Kat was not one to lead him on, something even before falling for Natalie, he hadn't had a like of. He liked honesty and he was getting it from the beautiful, strong lady he loved.

"I get it," he said. "What if we say we just take it one day at a time? Isn't that what normal people do, people who haven't ever felt loss?"

He could almost see her thoughts rolling in her expression, then she looked at him in a way that twisted him on the inside, a hopeful way. "One day at a time. Yes, let's try that. Before I lost my friend, I had dreams. I just found out how things change."

He breathed an internal breath. "Great, would you like to go for a walk outside of your restaurant?" He wanted to be with her with no one watching.

She smiled. "I think that's a perfect idea. I know a perfect place down the street to get some sweet treats or ice cream."

He smiled, relieved and happy. "Now we're talking ice cream I know things are getting serious." He stood and she did too then told the waitress they could close up and led the way out of the restaurant by the sea.

The moment they walked out of the parking lot and she turned left and headed toward the smaller tourist filled area along the bay. Music drifted from several restaurants, hers included behind them as they headed toward new ground for them to walk together on.

"I love the art stores and the walk along the bay's stone wall here," she said as they joined the other people walking down the street, enjoying the night.

The lights along the main stretch glowed on the water as they walked along the sidewalk by the water. Across the road were the two-story restaurants and bars mixed in with the jewelry stores, shops to choose from when they reached steps that led up to stores on their side of the water. Kat stopped at an art store. It was closed this late, but she paused and looked in the window. He stopped beside her, their arms touching.

"So you've been here working for my dad for how many months?"

"About six."

"And you've not come and walked around town before?" She looked up at him.

"No. I haven't. I stay at the ranch. I mean, I go into Waimea a lot. It's a nice town."

"Yes. It is. But it's a cowboy town and has great food and feed stores." She grinned. "Everything you'd find in a regular good old Texas town full of cattlemen."

He laughed. "You've got that right. I guess that's why I'm comfortable there."

"I guess. I used to love it too. But even when I loved

it, I liked getting away here to this tourist phenomenon."

"I understand why. It's nice."

She started walking, he fell into step with her, his arm brushed hers and the want to hold her hand was strong. He'd even thought about what it would be like to kiss her. That thought he'd been dealing with because he hadn't wanted to kiss anyone since losing Natalie.

He stopped walking and she did too. They were now in front of a walkway before the other restaurants that were very busy on this side of the road, the end of town, actually. It was busier and many had already crossed over to be there, but here they were still in a quiet area.

"Clay," she said looking up at him. And to his surprise she lifted her hand and cupped his face and then she leaned in and kissed him.

Emotion roared through him as the feel of her lips, the touch of her hand overtook him. The atmosphere of her knowing that this is what he wanted filled him. Unable to stop himself, he gently wrapped his arms around her as if she were a fine piece of china, and he was afraid to break her. She took a step into his arms, and he held her close as they continued kissing.

And then he lifted his face from hers and looked into her beautiful eyes, her auburn hair brushing his arms. "I haven't done that in a long time."

"I haven't either. I know. I'm single, never been married. Never lost the love of my life. Just my friend. But I can't believe I just kissed you like that. I did what I've been afraid of doing."

"Afraid of kissing someone?" he was shocked by that.

"Yes. Kissing someone is the beginning of opening your heart. You know?"

Oh, yes, he knew. As he looked at her now, he knew exactly how kissing someone opened a heart. His heart was raging and he now knew that he had already fallen in love with this wonderful woman.

She broke the kiss and stepped away. "So there we have that out of the way. Don't think I'm going to kiss you all the time, cowboy. I just thought we needed to get it out of the way. I *am* a take-charge kind of woman."

He laughed with relief. The woman knew exactly what he was experiencing, or she was a person who knew how to read people. "You are a take-charge kind of lady and I love y—it," he said, relieved by her kiss and that he'd caught himself before saying he loved her. "I have to say, for our first kiss, I hope it's not our last kiss."

She hitched her auburn brow. "I guess that means we'll have to walk down the street together again, *or* maybe I could take a step forward and come out to the ranch, and we can go riding the hills. Not the ones we rode last time? This time I think we need to be focused on what's going on between us."

"I agree. How about tomorrow?"

"I have a major online meeting tomorrow. But how about the next day?" He couldn't help it, he reached out and took her hand in his. It felt as perfect as he'd thought it would, and then she curled her fingers around his and it was right.

"Well, since you work for my dad on our ranch, and if I interrupt your business dealings, that means I'll be interrupting my dad's business meetings too. I think you're right, day after tomorrow works great."

"I can't wait to go riding along the hillsides with

you and show you some of the updates we've made."

"I'll love that. On that call you have tomorrow, is my dad going to be involved in that call?"

"Actually, no."

"Good. I hope you're not planning on calling him and telling him that I kissed you and that we're going riding tomorrow." She lifted that eyebrow again.

That eyebrow that he enjoyed watching hitch upward. "No, I'm not." Suddenly it slammed into him and he dropped her hand. "I'm not the other guy. I don't have to work at your dad's ranch. I'm not the hired hand looking for a step up. I can walk away from the job tonight if you need that reassurance."

"No, but thanks for the update." She smiled. "I was teasing. I only need you to be you. That was the other guy—I would have never walked out here with you or kissed you if I'd have even thought something like that."

He reached for her hand that met his instantly. "Then we have a plan for day after tomorrow."

"Perfect," she said. And he agreed.

CHAPTER TWELE

Kat drove to the ranch early two days after she kissed the cowboy.

Now, heart thundering, she drove up the lane to the ranch house. It was an amazingly beautiful place sitting here on the mountain with a view, not of the calm waters she loved but of the rough waters and volcanos on the other side of the island. Her dad always said he'd built the house with this view because he knew challenge had two looks, this side of the mountain showed the threat of eruption—but also showed the amazing beauty of the orange glow if given the space it required.

Now, driving up the drive for the first time in a long time, Kat's heart raced with so many thoughts.

Memories of strength she saw in her sweet friend Olivia now. Her quiet beautiful friend who'd known her like no other, seeing in her that she wasn't as strong as she tried to make everyone think she was. The note told her that in its own way, that Olivia suspected that and one day might need a reminder.

Her mind rolling with memories, she pulled to a halt in the driveway and spotted the handsome, take-my-breath-away cowboy walk out of the house to greet her.

She let the feeling she wasn't used to feeling rage through her as he beat her to the door and opened it for her.

What was she doing? That question raged through her as she got out and looked at him. The man she hadn't been able to get off her mind since kissing him.

"Welcome home. I'm glad to see you." He reached out then and touched her face, his gaze drilling into hers. "I've had you on my mind ever since we walked down the sidewalk."

"Right back at you." Heart racing and knowing she wanted to kiss him again, she stepped back. "I haven't been here in years."

"I know. That's why I said let's meet here. I thought you would want to see the place. We keep it up while your parents aren't here. My office is actually attached to my place, which is part of the horse stalls."

She smiled, startled by his words. "You live in my favorite place. The apartment above the horse stalls."

"Your favorite? The horse stalls or the apartment?"

"I love the stalls, but I love the apartment too. I had actually thought one day that would be my apartment. Of course, I wanted to upgrade it. Did Dad upgrade it for you?"

He smiled at this. "Actually, after I moved here he told me to make it mine and I did. Your dad even told me I could live in the main house if I wanted to, but I wasn't doing that. Besides that, the moment I walked into the apartment I loved it. I did a few small renovations and that's all. I liked it too much."

"I would love to see all that you've done there, but let's go in here first. I haven't been home in so long, I know that Dad would want me to be inside looking around."

Clay grinned. "So you really are trying to make

148

your dad feel good because, yes, he would actually like you coming in the main house for a visit." He opened the large, warm, varnished oak door and let her enter first. The entrance hall was beautiful, there was no denying it. Obviously, her parents had gone to great extent to make it a welcoming family place and he had a feeling they hoped to one day have grandchildren visiting here for vacations.

If he hadn't been so intent on having his own place, then he would have enjoyed living here. The doorway opened into the huge living space, but also if you stepped to the right you were in the beautiful kitchen area next. That was where Kat went smiling. She stopped at the large island. "This is my favorite spot. My mom is amazing in the kitchen and would have been a wonderful chef if she'd chosen to do that. She chose a family and I'm so glad I got to learn from her. I got my want to be a chef from standing here with her in this room, where Chef Mom instigated the creations I came up with."

He smiled, seeing her here as a young girl and teen. And now. She looked at peace, and this was a perfect spot for her. "I see it. Are you sure you weren't just sitting at the bar watching your mom cook?" He couldn't help teasing her.

"I was beside her as soon as I could walk. We made a chocolate cake." She smiled. "She couldn't cook without me trying to help."

"One day you could have a little girl or maybe boy or both of your own wanting you to help them cook." She would be a wonderful mother.

She looked at him, her hands on her slim hips. "Let's go on in to the next room." She headed toward the entrance to the family room. It too was large, wide open, leather couches, brown and cream, and a gigantic fireplace made from the same cream and yellow and tan stones from outside. She walked to the fireplace. "I don't know if you know, but my dad actually made that mantle. Me, Pearl, and Dora went with him to search for the right tree in the woods. When we found it he went to work on it the minute we got it to the barn. It's something he enjoyed doing. Who knows, he might start doing it again when he and Mom get grandkids and stay home a little more. But right now, they are living Mom's dream and traveling all over the world."

"That's what he told me when he told me to move in here. Said they would be traveling places they hadn't been, so that meant Kona was off the list for a little while. Unless one of his girls decided to move back to the ranch. But you haven't."

She crossed her arms and looked around. "I haven't because of, well, things that I didn't want to get into. But after we went out the other day and saw what Olivia had left me, I have been thinking about everything. My sisters and my brother have all embraced family. And though it scares me, it has been on my mind lately."

Their gazes were locked and Clay's heart quickened. Did he have anything to do with that? He didn't ask, however, the curiosity inside him was overwhelming and knowing now that he wanted to have something to do with her choosing to come back home. That realization was stronger than anything had ever been.

"When I walked into this big, beautiful family room the first time," he said, unable not to. "It threw me for a loop because it reminded me of what I'd lost. Natalie and I had dreamed of one day having a large home to raise our kids in. A dream home to raise a family in."

She shifted from boot to boot and he stopped talking knowing he was making her uncomfortable. He'd spoken when he shouldn't have but he hadn't thought about this for a long while. It was an added grief that went with losing Natalie.

"So, you dreamed of having a house full of kids too." It wasn't a question from Kat in her soft voice but an acknowledgement from his words that she understood.

"As we both know, life changes the way you think."

She nodded. "Yes, when Olivia died, my life desires changed."

"I understand. But, I have to be honest, there is no denying that meeting you has opened my eyes to maybe thinking about that again." His heart exploded. He'd felt Natalie's push on the boat that day of fishing. Of letting go and urging him on and now as he stared at the strong, caring with all her heart Kat, he wanted that life again.

"Are you ready to go for a ride?" he asked, needing space before he messed up. He needed to get away from the thoughts he was thinking. This is good.

"Let's go for a ride," she said instantly and headed toward the door as if needing the space as much as he did.

She led the way through the kitchen, the hallway, and then the back entryway, where boots had their place after a rough day if needed, before going further inside. They walked past it all and out the door and she didn't hesitate but led the way across the wide-open land toward the stables. The two-story metal building was home to the horses below and him on the second level.

As he followed Kat he knew that on this day, Clay felt he had the ability to maybe change his life forever if everything worked out.

But all of that depended on Kat. He was already on board, in all the way.

* * *

Kat's mind roared as they crossed the drive to the place where she had thought she would live one day. The place where she could have her own spot, live on the ranch, still have restaurants like she dreamed. Her plan had been to make the drive into town a couple of times a week and use her apartment on the ocean when needed.

She entered the long, wide alley that ran straight through the huge building with horse stalls on both sides. Wooden and metal combined to make a beautiful place for the amazing horses that belonged to her family. Walking into the space was like a breath of fresh air. Air that reminded her why she was a cowgirl at heart. Peace like a river flowed over her, enveloping her in its fast-running stream.

It was gorgeous. She focused on the stalls and the majestic heads of horses now looking over their gates at her. She smiled. "Hello, everyone, Kat's here." Instantly she saw ears go to attention and whinnies let loose throughout the barn.

"I think they're glad to see you and hear your beautiful voice," Clay said, stopping beside her. She felt his nearness as if it was a hug waiting to happen.

A hug she wanted to happen.

"That makes me happy. I've missed them too." She

looked up above at the wooden second story that had windows that looked down over the stall area. It also had windows on the other side that overlooked the pastures from above. And a beautiful deck that was her favorite. She couldn't help it. "Do you still have the big deck on the back? You didn't do away with that I hope."

"No way, it's amazing. The best view of the horse pastures, the rolling hills and valleys and the beautiful islands across the wide-open ocean all in one picturesque packed back deck." He grinned. "I'd be an idiot if I got rid of that."

"I love it that way too."

"I spend many hours out there on that deck. Do you want to go see it?"

"I would love to. I actually helped my dad design that area up there."

"Really? Now that I know that I see your hand in it. Like putting the topping on a dish, the open windows out to the deck is your added touch. Wide open and inspiring."

She smiled feeling warm inside that he knew her. "Exactly."

"Well, come on up." They walked to the inside stairway then he stood back and let her lead the way. It had this one and then another one from the private back deck, which also had a private place to park beneath it.

It was just a beautiful, wide open home place that she loved. Her heart welled thinking about all the things that were coming to her as they walked up the stairs. When she reached the platform that was the area where the railings led to the door, she let Clay pass by to open the door since it was his place now. He moved past her, then pushed the door wide.

"After you," he said, standing close.

"Thank you, sir," she drawled and walked into the room. It was a simple entrance with the beautiful wooden floors that had been from the trees on Kona, sanded and varnished and still glistened with beauty as she walked into the room. Some of the walls had the same varnished wooden appeal.

And then, of course, stucco painted cream tones. She followed the hallway when she walked into the living room, she just stopped short. He stood beside her as she took in the wide-open view across the room through the huge window showing the deck then the pastures and onto the amazingly blue waters of the ocean.

"I love this view," she said, breathless. "I always couldn't wait to get here after a long day."

He looked at her, clearly stunned. "Exactly. So, you came here to the apartment at the end of a day? Did you live here?"

"I did for a very short time. Before Olivia died, I'd moved in here, and I drove down the hillsides to my restaurant on a daily basis. I did have my apartment still. And on really busy days, I stayed there."

"I didn't know that."

Totally shocked her father hadn't told him that he was remodeling his daughter's place. Kat frowned. "I can't believe Dad didn't tell you."

"I'm sorry," he said, seriously. "If I changed anything in here that you wanted to keep, I'll make it right."

"No." She led the way into the kitchen that overlooked the living space. "You didn't do a lot but I like the upgrades I see. The main attraction that I see you didn't touch are the beautiful wooden floors from our land. And the windows are amazing, but the deck is my favorite after the kitchen and as far as I can tell you didn't change anything in here."

He grinned. "You're right. When I walked into the kitchen, I didn't think it needed any updating. It's beautiful. Kind of like the big house. Soft light wood and amazing cookware."

She laughed. "The cookware wins the day. This was the place I lived when going to the Hawai'i Community College of Culinary Arts to become a chef. I drove the hour and a half each day to Hilo on the other side of the island then came back here each night. I loved those days and nights learning my craft and when I graduated I got my first job in Kona. Then went home to Texas and took classes from many great chefs that I admired. I couldn't help myself, I loved time in the kitchen and though I loved the ranch, cooking was my dream. So, I talked Dad into making an investment in my restaurant, that I paid back in full, and my career was born there on the coast of Star Gazer Island. I was the total age of twenty-two when I opened Café By The

Seaside. And blessed that it was an instant success."

He smiled. "Blessed with talent for the flair for cooking that set you apart."

She grinned. "Okay, yes, I have a way that I do things that I think does set my places apart but so do many others."

"I like that you don't have a big head. So you started here in this kitchen."

"Yes, in my mom's kitchen with her was where it started but then here in this place was where I found my place. My way, overlooking the ocean. This is where I got much of my inspiration, looking out that huge window over that blue water."

"So you knew that young that this was where you wanted to live. Make this your home place? On that mountainside you talked to Olivia about those children you wanted to bring up here. Did you want to feed them the fantastic meals you make?"

Their gazes locked. "Yes."

He leaned against the counter, crossed his arm. "I actually like this story. You knew and know what you want. You've worked really hard to accomplish it. I see that, but there's more to this I think."

"I think in that we are alike. You also knew what you wanted at an early age. You wanted to be a rancher, then you fell in love, not with a cowgirl like most would think but instead you fell for a woman who was a champion fisherman." She smiled. "And for a while, you had it all."

His gaze dimmed then he nodded. "Yes. That's why you understand where I'm at. I know what I want and what I don't want to lose. Or thought I did." He pushed himself away from the counter and took two steps toward her, placed his hands on each of her upper arms gently. "I'm seeing right now the strength of the woman in front of me who was and is driven for what she wants. I love that. But you need to go after what you truly want. No fear."

She tingled through and through with the feel of his hands on her. The look in his eyes. "You go after what you love too."

His lips lifted into a smile. "I do. That's why I'm wondering why you have left out half of your dream. The one we talked about the other day on the side of the mountain. The conversation you so easily just sidestepped."

The man was not going where she was trying to keep him away from. Her conversation with Olivia on the mountainside. They were having such a good time, he'd actually had her wanting him to lean forward and kiss her.

Emotions ripped through her. He'd gone to the subject she didn't want or need to go to. His blue eyes dug deep and she gave in. "Yes, I once wanted family and spoke to Olivia about it. But life changes. Dreams change." His hold was gentle and she could pull away but she couldn't move, her heart kept her feet planted beside his.

"I think you have a weak spot, that is, you're afraid to face having the family that you dreamed of here on this island, on this ranch, overlooking the water and the bay. I think you still want it but you're hiding out from it because of losing Olivia. You were the strong one and wouldn't ever let anyone know just how hard your loss hurt."

Her insides clenched. Tears threatened her eyes.

She blinked them away. Wanted to step back, shrug him off, stomp out of the building. Instead, she held those amazing eyes with hers. Somehow she knew this cowboy saw everything. "You get it, cowboy. But what we've talked about is just between you and me. You've seen my weakness from losing her was for me. But the one thing for sure is we can't always have everything we want. Or wanted."

"You're right. We can't." He dropped his hands and then strode toward the door leading out onto the deck, and she followed.

Something in his eyes had called to her.

CHAPTER THIRTEEN

Clay was feeling openly startled by everything he'd just realized. He'd seen similarities in Natalie and Kat. Between these two, but not that many, which he was glad of, glad they were still separated by unique things. And yet, what they had in common wasn't just their beauty inside and out, but it was their determination. Their drive to do what they wanted to do, the way they wanted to do it. In Natalie, he'd learned it early on but loved her anyway for it. If she couldn't fish in her own eyes she was no one, so fishing was her life. He had never been certain they'd have the kids he'd wanted. He didn't and had never let himself dwell on that truth but right now it was here wrapped around him like thin wire cutting slowly through him.

Natalie had dropped everything when she realized she wanted to be a competitive fisherman. Her father had been able to give her some help. From there on, she had made it on her own. She had moved close to the water, worked on boats so she was able to go fishing when she could and learn from everything she saw while working on the boats. And she'd learned from some of the best fishermen out there, even helped them reel in fish and got paid for doing it. And then she went out, and she started catching for herself. Got noticed, sponsored, and she built from there.

This lady now standing on this beautiful upper deck that overlooked the bay had done the same in many ways. And he knew that was part of the deep attraction he felt toward her. It didn't matter who or what was said or done. She went for what her heart drove her to do.

He put his hands on the banister of the porch and looked out over the water, not at the woman beside him who had a grip on his heart, and he knew it.

He'd only ever felt that grip once, and he'd never wanted to feel that grip again. But he knew right now, it was there. But could he risk losing again, and maybe not having any children with which to remember her by if something ever did happen? That was his greatest regret with Natalie, having no children to carry on their love.

"Kat, I love your drive," he managed, through almost gritted teeth.

She came to stand beside him and chose to have her shoulder touching his. Electric vibes raced between them, the sensation had him wanting to forget everything and turn and pull her into his arms. His grip on the railing held him back. He couldn't ask her to do what her heart wasn't going to let her do. He didn't need that either.

"This deck, that water, this place, you have now," she said softly, then she turned to face him. "You've brought life back here. You've giving it what it needs. I think it's giving you what you need too. And you've given my dad relief being able to let him know I'm okay. I'm thankful for that."

"But," he said.

She placed her hand on his chest. "I'm just going to tell you. I'm thankful for what you've inspired in me. I see what I left behind. I see what Olivia knew I left behind and what she knew I would need. Somehow, I see it all when we talk and when I'm near you. Does that scare you?"

Unable to stop himself, he wrapped his arms gently around her and pulled her close. Felt emotions sweep through him as she leaned her head onto his chest and wrapped her arms around him and held on tight.

"Kat, I was afraid too. I didn't want to ever take a chance on feeling what I've felt since losing Natalie. But now, I did for you, Kat, I have opened my heart. I'm praying that this doesn't scare you away, but I can't deny that I love you."

She looked up at him and kissed him. Her arms clutched tightly and her kiss was amazing and full of everything he hoped for. There was no denying that he loved this strong woman who had opened up to him like she had not opened up to anyone else.

He was grateful that God had put him here, had given him this moment to be here with her, in this time.

"I feel so much when I'm with you," she said. "And when we talk I really open up," she paused, "Clay, I think we could fall in love."

He grinned. "Darl'n, I already love you, but I'll wait as long as you want me to because I know I had never expected it to be two in a lifetime that I could love so much. And if you get that, then you are the one for me. And I will wait forever until you tell me there's no hope and to leave you alone and get the heck off of this island."

She laughed. "Oh my goodness. You, cowboy, can take me from tears to laughter. I am amazed that you love me, and I…"

"You don't have to say it. I get it. You're hesitant. Saying those words is a commitment you are not sure you can make. So let's give this up right now and do like we had planned to do. Let's go for a horse ride, and then you go back to town and cook. I know that's where your heart is and your thoughts are. Come on." Taking no chances, he took her hand and led the way down the stairs and to the horses.

And he prayed that if it was God's will, this sweet, beautiful, amazing woman would have fallen in love with him too. And when it was time, it would be time.

* * *

They wasted no time going down and picking out their horses. Kat's heart was roaring, her mind going crazy. And she knew she hadn't thought in a million years that she'd make this decision, but even thinking about making a decision or taking a chance on falling in love wasn't a choice. She loved this man. This man who was trying to give her time, trying not to rush her.

And she loved that.

They were on their horses and riding through the pastures within moments. Kat knew she'd once dreamed of the man who would ride beside her over the mountains and valleys of their land and life. She'd given that up but here he was and it felt so right.

He'd lost what he thought was the love of his life, only to realize that God made hearts bigger and wider than we each believe. He loved her and he loved Natalie and it was so clear, and so very dear.

Her brother Matt knew the same emotions of love, loss, and loving again. And Kat had been a chicken, a tough gal on the outside for everyone but not for herself.

Until now.

"You are an amazing man, cowboy," she said, when they topped the hillside and she halted Ladybug.

"No. I'm not. I'm just a guy who knows that there is a miracle happening around him right now. A miracle in that love can overcome everything. Love can take you through everything, put you through everything, but it's something worth every moment. You only take a chance when you know it's right, and, Kat, I'm looking at you, and know that me loving you is right. But no pressure."

"How do you make it sound so easy?"

"It isn't easy. It is a commitment. Commitment to love someone with all your heart in the good times and the hard times. Happy and sad times. And I did that once, and cherish it. But now I'm praying that you feel the same and will let me love and cherish you. I never thought it could happen again, love. But it's here."

Kat loved this man. She gently pulled her horse's reins and Ladybug stepped sideways so that her and Clay's legs touched. Then Kat reached with her hand as he leaned toward her and her hand connected with his neck, then she gently pulled his lips to hers and they kissed—she could kiss this cowboy forever.

Oh, the blessing, the feeling that went through her in that moment because everything in the kiss promised things that she had thought she'd never feel or have. Against his lips, she said, "Clay, I love you and want this to be us always."

He pulled back. "This, as in me and you married and in love watching our kids play here on this mountain pasture over the sea?"

She smiled with her heart. "Yes, exactly. I'm ready to start an amazing life with you." She was tearing up. "I want to be your wife."

"And have a herd of kids with me?"

"Yes, as many as God will grant us."

Clay was off his horse in that instant and was beside her as he lifted her from the saddle and into her arms. "I love you, Kat, and I always will. Let's get our life together started."

She cupped his face. "On this mountainside is where I want to say 'I do'."

"That sounds perfect to me." And then he lowered his lips to hers and they kissed... and would forever more.

EPILOGUE

Kat smiled at her sisters standing there on the hilltop overlooking the ocean with the bench where sweet Olivia had left her the note of her lifetime. They were smiling at her. She was smiling at them. Her heart so full, so unbelievably full. Pearl shook her head.

"I still can't believe our dad was your matchmaker."

Dora chuckled. "Me either. But it's awesome to think when Clay showed up here, Dad had a hope and knew Clay needed to be here. God was the matchmaker."

Kat smiled. "Yes, He is. Our dad doesn't get mixed up in other people's business very much, but he knew that me and Clay could help each other. Sometimes that simple thing can change lives. It did ours."

She loved the man standing down the slope waiting for her dad to walk her to him.

As if on cue her dad came over as the music started. "Are you ready?"

She smiled up at him. "Yes. I'm so ready."

Pearl and Dora came together, and they embraced her.

"This is a great day and it's going to be a great life," she said, hugging them tightly. She now knew that whatever life held for her from this moment on was in God's hands.

She prayed that she got to live a long life with the man waiting for her at the altar but would be grateful for every moment. His gaze met hers, and that unbelievable smile of his radiated into her heart.

Like sweet Olivia had said, *Be grateful for every moment.*

She would be forever grateful. "I'm ready, Dad. My matchmaking father."

He smiled down at her. "Believe me, Kat, I only

prayed God would help my tough gal with the soft heart. And He knew what you needed. Who you needed. I'm excited for the future you're going to build here, you and Clay, and that herd of grandkids he told me was coming. The ones that are going to be playing on this hillside one day."

Kat's heart jumped with excitement thinking of her and Clay's children and her brother's and sisters' too.

"Let's do this. I'm so ready to get this party started."

Her sisters walked together down the hillside, past all the people who were here to cheer them on. They took their place across from their husbands, who were standing beside Clay. And then she and her dad walked down that hill past the bench where Olivia had left her secret letter, giving her the strength and the knowledge of knowing that there was more to life than dying. Life itself was such a gift. There on the bench was a flower arrangement and her lunchbox with the smiling face on it.

She smiled. Life with someone you loved was an amazing gift. Short or long, the timespan for everyone was unknown, but each moment was what we made of it. What she and Clay would make of it.

Kat was smiling and knew from above that Natalie and Olivia were smiling as her father handed her hand over to Clay. Her man placed his warm, strong hand around hers and squeezed gently. She smiled like the sun over the blue waters behind them and knew that her life was just beginning, and what a life it was going to be.

About the Author

Debra Clopton is a USA Today bestselling & International bestselling author who has sold over 3.5 million books. She has published over 81 books under her name and her pen name of Hope Moore.

Under both names she writes clean & wholesome and inspirational, small town romances, especially with cowboys but also loves to sweep readers away with romances set on beautiful beaches surrounded by topaz water and romantic sunsets.

Her books now sell worldwide and are regulars on the Bestseller list in the United States and around the world. Debra is a multiple award-winning author, but of all her awards, it is her reader's praise she values most. If she can make someone smile and forget their worries for a few hours (or days when binge reading one of her series) then she's done her job and her heart is happy. She really loves hearing she kept a reader from doing the dishes or sleeping!

A sixth-generation Texan, Debra lives on a ranch in Texas with her husband surrounded by cattle, deer, very busy squirrels and hole digging wild hogs. She enjoys traveling and spending time with her family.

Visit Debra's website and sign up for her newsletter
for updates at: www.debraclopton.com

Check out her Facebook at:
www.facebook.com/debra.clopton.5

Follow her on Instagram at: debraclopton_author

or contact her at debraclopton@ymail.com